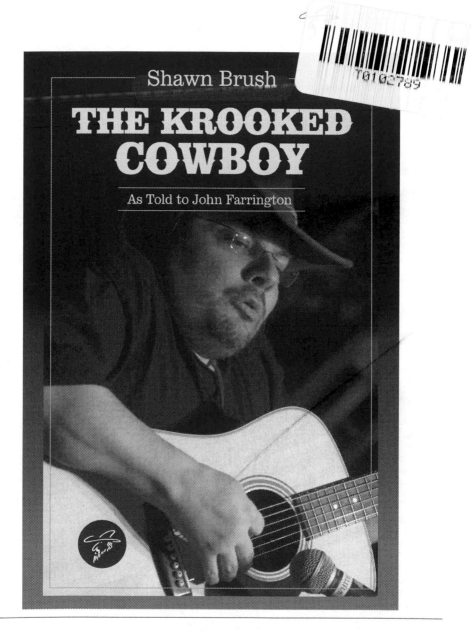

Shawn Brush

# THE KROOKED COWBOY

As Told to John Farrington

Published by

**farrington**media

in co-operation with

**Trafford**
PUBLISHING™

Order this book online at www.trafford.com
or email orders@trafford.com

Most Trafford titles are also available at major online book retailers.

Note for Librarians: A cataloguing record for this book is available from Library
and Archives Canada at www.collectionscanada.ca/amicus/index-e.html

Printed in Victoria, BC, Canada.

ISBN: 978-1-4251-8342-4 (Soft)
ISBN: 978-1-4269-1637-3 (Hard)
ISBN: 978-1-4251-8344-8 (e-book)

*Our mission is to efficiently provide the world's finest, most comprehensive
book publishing service, enabling every author to experience success.
To find out how to publish your book, your way, and have it available
worldwide, visit us online at www.trafford.com*

*Trafford rev. 9/4/2009*

 www.trafford.com

**North America & international**
toll-free: 1 888 232 4444 (USA & Canada)
phone: 250 383 6864 ♦ fax: 812 355 4082

# DEDICATION

This book is dedicated to the people who mean the most to me.

My mother and father. For always being there giving me support and guidance. Allowing me to be myself and chase my dreams. I don't think I always expressed my Love and appreciation for them at times. This is my way of saying thank you mom and dad for everything. Without your support I would not have done the things I have done.

I would also like to dedicate it to all the Little People of the world and anyone who has ever been affected by Morquio.

Shawn Brush

The Krooked Cowboy

# TABLE OF CONTENTS

Kyle Weir photo

**66**

**When I first saw Shawn performing his music I thought this was a special young man with outstanding talent. As I watched, his incredible feel for his acoustic guitar matched with his strong and heartfelt voice, drew me into his songs like a magnet. The depth of emotion evident in his songs can only mold the listener into a fan, the fan into a believer, and the believer into a companion on his journey through the 'land of giants.'**

**99**

*Ray Materick*

# ACKNOWLEDGMENTS

There are so many people I can think of that it's hard to know where to start. If I list every single name I would have another book!!!

First I'd like to thank you the reader for purchasing this book. I hope you enjoy it and can share it with others.

My close friends and family for always being there through thick and thin.

To all my musical friends and peers, you still inspire me!

My heroes for being examples and to my fans that keep me wanting to do more.

And a special 'thank you' to all those who helped with the proofreading, editing and transcribing: Lynda Henriksen, Terance Howell, Anne-Marie Farrington, Sarah Banks, Adair Thompson, Michaele Lowachee and Carol Mondragon.

# ACKNOWLEDGMENTS

Kyle Weir has been taking photographs at my concerts for a number of years. Several of the photographs in this book, including the one chosen for the cover, are Kyle's work. See more of Kyle's photos at www.kyleweir.zenfolio.com

It is images like these that earned him the distinction of Photographer of the Year at the 2006 and the 2007 Hamilton Music Awards.

Kyle was raised and educated in Hamilton, Ontario, but it wasn't until his mid-thirties, and on his way to his father's homeland of Scotland, that he found his mode of creative expression - the camera. After a couple years of obsessive focus on how to create a meaningful image, his work started to be recognized and published in books, magazines, and newspapers.

"Perhaps my most meaningful images, are those of my musician friends" says Kyle about his work with the local Hamilton music scene. "I try to hold still moments of the artist's creative expression."

He has been privileged to work alongside such incredible artists including the likes of Daniel Lanois and Garth Hudson . . . and The Krooked Cowboy says he is really thankful - even flattered - that Kyle has devoted so much time to capture him in concert.

KYLE WEIR

www.kyleweir.zenfolio.com

Publication design: farringtonmedia, Oakville, Ontario

www.ANDREWtheARTIST.com, Brussels, Belgium

Cover design: Jason Collins, Brand/Bite,

Published by

**farrington**media

2007 Erika Court

Oakville, Ontario, Canada, L6M 4R4

Tel. 905-469-4201 Fax: 1-866-265-9122

email: john@farringtonmedia.com www.farringtonmedia.com

in co-operation with

 Trafford
PUBLISHING

2657 Wilfert Road, Victoria, B.C., Canada, V9B 5Z3

info@trafford.com     www.trafford.com

Shawn Brush at Hamilton's Staircase Theatre in 2004 . . . the Dreamcatcher made its first appearance at this one-man concert.

# INTRODUCTION

By John Farrington

S hawn Brush is one in a million.

Just looking at him you know he is different than your average man.

Listen to one of his CDs and you'll be pleased with what you hear.

When you learn that he has written most of the songs he sings you'll wonder why you haven't heard more about him.

Meet him and you'll be amazed with his abilities, his positive outlook on life, his dry wit.

Get to know him and you'll be impressed by his love of life and drive for perfection.

Give it a week or two and you'll uncover the real treasure – a genuine friend. He expects nothing, but gives all.

Assisting him with the compilation of this autobiography has been a lesson in life.

Shawn was born with Morquio's disease, one of the rare causes of dwarfism.

He pushes four-feet in height, but has long believed that size doesn't matter. In fact, we looked at that and other titles for the book that played on his height.

He's not squeamish about the fact that he is a little person, but he emphatically doesn't want to go through life playing on the sensitivities of others. He wants to succeed on his own merit.

In his case he wants to be known as a singer, a song writer or a guitarist, not solely for his size.

When he was trying to get established in the recording industry a few years ago he sent away a CD to try to get a contract with a major label in Canada. They sent him  back a note saying they liked his music, but indicating he needed a gimmick!

Shawn thought that was a great joke. Lesser men may have sent back a picture of themselves. Shawn though is true to himself. He is determined to succeed on his musical talent that he is developing, rather than on the shape of the body he has been given.

# Introduction

It is not going to be easy to succeed. His condition prevents him from taking his music to the public to get as much publicity as up-and-coming stars need.

Shawn's world is about a 100 kilometre radius around his hometown of Burlington, Ontario. Any farther afield than that and he struggles with energy and health.

He has never been on tour. In fact, he finds it difficult to play two nights in a row even close to his home, sleeping in his own bed every night.

His music and his family and friends are his life. His medical condition is the dominating factor in all that he does . . . but he doesn't play on it. He knows he has to take care of himself or even the restricted life he does have now would be further curtailed.

Here is a man who has known his limits all his life. He hasn't been afraid to push them at times, and still does. He just knows that very fine line between being well and being sick and is smart enough to listen to his body when it's telling him enough is enough.

He longs for the day that he might find a life-long partner.

He has struggled through the teen years watching friends of both sexes grow up, get married, settle down and have children. He has had many lady friends in his life, some have even touched his heart – a few perhaps not knowing the heartache he suffered as they left his life. Some of them perhaps not knowing how much he wished they were still a part of his life.

As gregarious, humourous, confident, caring – and occasionally outspoken – as he is around his friends, when it comes to the tender most feelings of his heart he is not a kiss and tell guy.

This autobiography, which started off back in 2003 with a working title of *Up Until Now,* is far from over. At this stage he has chosen not to mention any of the women who have been a part of his life at various times since his teens. Respect him for that. There is nothing untoward about any of these relationships – and there have been one or two that could have developed, that he wished would have continued.

He was contacted at one time by the Sally Jessy Raphael show to go on a blind date in New York. He refused. They came back several times to try to persuade him to go on a date with someone in New York City. They were willing to pay his airfare, put him up in a hotel and pay all other expenses.

What he would have to give up would be his privacy.

# The Krooked Cowboy

Shawn saw this as a story that had little value other than base entertainment. He does not regard himself as anything other than a regular person in a smaller body.

He felt the TV show would have exploited him and the other person involved. As much as the multi-million television audience may have given his career a huge boost, it was totally against all the principles of good taste, honesty and respect that he treasures most in life.

He is a man of his word. And that matters to Shawn.

He is different than most of us.

But don't base that difference just on the way he looks.

You are in for a very pleasant surprise.


Sincerely,


John Farrington

Editor and Publisher

April 2009


*John Farrington has been a journalist for 50 years, starting in his English hometown weekly in Crewe, Cheshire, in July 1958. He worked in England for seven years before emigrating to Canada in 1965. He has been Managing Editor at several Canadian newspapers, including Kirkland Lake, Peterborough, Sarnia, Lethbridge, and Sudbury and Publisher and General Manager in Nanaimo, Timmins. Cornwall and the Multicom group in Toronto. He was National Editorial Consultant for Thomson Newspapers from 1980-1982 and Northern Ontario Journalist of the Year in 1990. He collaborated with Stompin' Tom Connors on his Number 1 autobiography. Currently he operates his own company, farringtonmedia, publishing, editing and writing books, and produces a quarterly in-flight magazine for Air Creebec, serving the Cree communities in the James Bay area of Ontario and Quebec.*

To Shawn Bush interested parties,

I've known Shawn for over 10 years. His songs have touched my heart they resonate truth and dedication.

I have to assume that Shawn's honesty, and imagination, would make their way into whatever project he decides to go after.

The little dude with a big heart, gets my vote.

In support

Daniel Lanois

X

I have always had a lot of respect for Daniel Lanois - and you can imagine how I felt about him when I received this letter.

# FOREWORD

By Shawn Brush

I love life. But it is a constant pain for me. I don't know what it is like to be without pain. I have had very few pain-free days in my 38 years on this earth.

I say this not to evoke any sympathy or even empathy. I say it simply to set up this story in its true perspective and to also have you understand that being a little person (dwarf, midget, call it what you will), is not being a mini-you. I am not just a regular, normal person in a body half the size of an averaged-sized person.

Being small is not a regular life from a lower-to-the-ground perspective.

It is not being a man in a child's body.

It is more like being a young man in an old man's body . . . a body, even in the early years of childhood, that was breaking down at a rate far exceeding the normal body. When I was in my mid-20s, one doctor said I had the bones of an 85 year-old. That was more than 15 years ago!

I have written this book because I think I have a story to tell. You'll never get a better chance to walk in my shoes (and they are size five, by the way).

This isn't a pity me story, but maybe when you've been through these next couple of hundred pages you'll have an appreciation for what I go through – and what other little people face - in the daily battle to live as normal a life as possible.

I am different. But I am who I am. I will never be able to change the way I am. Don't ever think I wouldn't have liked to be a strapping six-footer with a wife, kids, job.

But I am happy in the body I am in.

My philosophy is that if you are going to work hard you may as well do something that you enjoy … and that is a better payment than a pay cheque.

Looking back on the past 15 years since I started playing music and making CDs I consider this has been my training … this is my university … this is my school of hard knocks. Eventually it is going to pay off, just the same as if I had gone to university.

# Foreword

I am learning from my experience and I have been amazed at the number of people, especially fellow musicians, who have helped me along the way. And, of course, nothing would have been possible without my mom and dad and my sister Michelle each putting up money for me to record my music and then make cassettes and CDs.

I owe my mom and dad more than anything and anybody. Financially and otherwise. Even though there were times in my life when I thought my mom was hard on me, I have realised as I grew older just how much my folks have sacrificed for me.

I always had a place to stay, food in the fridge, clean clothes and the use of the vehicle  - and they are genuinely proud of me and my accomplishments . . . and they continue to support me.

I have a feeling that I haven't really blossomed yet and, perhaps, writing this book will be my certificate, my degree, or my thesis, that will open up the door to independence a little wider. I often think how justice could be repaid if I am able to take care of my mom and dad in their years of need, just as they devoted and doted on me in all my years of need.

My hopes and dreams for the future don't involve hit records and millions of dollars in the bank. Independence for me can be achieved much more simply.

My big plan when I started the music, and still my number-one goal is to have a job where I can sustain myself and stand on my own two feet financially. It's still the goal.  Last year – 2007 – I had my best year yet. It involved a lot of busking outside the Liquor Store in Burlington, but it did provide me with a steady income that – while it reduced my disability pension – gave me the satisfaction of knowing that I was coming close to being able to sustain myself.

What I would like to see happen, sooner than later, of course, is a publishing deal, someone to help me sell my records or help my career.

Going on tour around the world, perhaps across Canada, even just in Ontario, would probably spark my career. But, of course, that depends on my staying healthy.

More realistic, I think, is to have other artists sing my songs.  That was one of my initial goals – and many people have sang them, but nothing big has happened yet.

If things started to take off in my music career, then I would be able to achieve some personal goals, which include building my own house and modifying it where it's comfortable with the counters at a level I could reach in the wheelchair.

In the immediate future I hope you have a chance to read this book and that it may help to inspire you to achieve your full potential.

Thanks for all your support over the years,


Shawn Brush

The Krooked Cowboy

March 2008

Robert Di Gioia talks with Shawn during the recording session for his latest CD, The Krooked Cowboy Rides Again. Robert produced it with Shawn and was also responsible for the mixing and the mastering.

# 'The Dude'

## who became

# 'THE KROOKED COWBOY'

. . . thanks to his creator.
*Shawn Brush*

# 1

# How I stole the Krooked Cowboy

I have to confess that I stole the name The Krooked Cowboy from a friend of mine, Ray Materick.

I had heard that Ray was going to call his group Ray Materick and the Crooked Cowboys. The name did something for me. I was out playing a gig in Brantford and I thought I would love to be a Crooked Cowboy.

So, on my way home from Brantford I stopped by Ray's home in Hamilton. He had not used the name yet so I thought I would ask him if he minded me using it. When I got to the house I said, "You know what, Ray, I am the Krooked Cowboy. I am officially stealing the name the Krooked Cowboy."

It was kind of a joke, but I started using it.

I put a K on crooked instead of C. That was to get away from the negative aspect of the word crooked.

It kind of stuck.

Once in a while Ray would say "I'm the Crooked Cowboy:" and he would steal back the name.

I'd say, "No I am the Krooked Cowboy,"

It was all in fun.

When a couple of people started calling me the Krooked Cowboy I realised that the name was beginning to stick.

# Shawn Brush

The Krooked Cowboy gets ready to ride again!

# The Krooked Cowboy

I rarely went out of the house without wearing a cowboy hat. I had been playing country and bluegrass songs all my life and I used to doodle and sketch a character I called The Dude.

When I drew The Dude wearing a cowboy hat there was no turning back on the name. I can draw The Dude really quickly and he has been my signature. Now he's The Krooked Cowboy.

It is a caricature and it is on my website.

The Dude is the Krooked Cowboy and I am the Krooked Cowboy. And now I think it is appropriate that I formally thank Ray for playing along with me and being such a good sport about it all.

Shawn with one of his heroes . . . Ray Materick.

I don't know what it is that attracted me to the name, I just thought it was me. It suited my persona. It fit my lifestyle. It was just what I needed to create the image I wanted to portray. It's worked. It's done all of these things for me. It has helped my career. At the same time it has not hindered Ray Materick's show biz career.

Unless you live in the Hamilton area, or are involved in the music scene in southern Ontario, chances are you have never heard of Ray Materick. However, you will be familiar with his song writing. One of his biggest was *Linda Put The Coffee On*, which made the Top 10 in the 70s.

Ray is a really great songwriter and I have even had the privilege of writing a couple of songs with him. He is really impressive as a songwriter, not to mention very prolific and quick. Everything he does is great. He has a lot of charisma.

It has been neat to know Ray because he's been right up there with a lot of the big guys, writing songs for the likes of Rompin' Ronnie Hawkins. While he still tours, he also helps others to polish their work.

# Shawn Brush

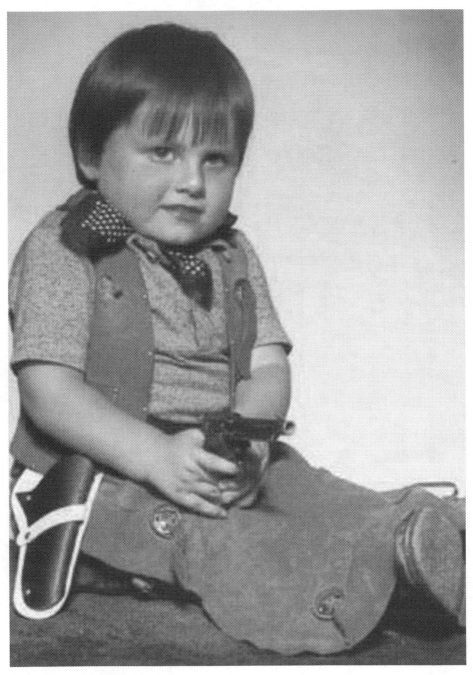

Shawn liked to be a Cowboy . . . even as a toddler.

# 2

# A normal childhood - except for all the pain

My childhood was probably like any other child's - except for the pain and the surgeries. You know, I can remember those early years just like it was yesterday - sitting in the pickup truck at the barn where we used to go horseback riding and listening to our 8-track.

We had the tapes of James Taylor, a couple of John Denver, and two of Willie Nelson's. Songs included James Taylor's *Fire and Rain*, John Denver's *Sunshine On My Shoulders* and, of course, Willie Nelson's *Phrases and Stages* album as well as his big album, *The Red-Headed Stranger*, which came out in the mid-70s. I would have been five or six years old.

I used to sit in the truck listening and singing along to the songs on those albums and we would talk about the fishing trips. We did a lot of fishing.

Dad would pick me up from school or we would go out late on a Friday night in the dark. We would leave from Burlington and my dad wouldn't touch a highway. We would go up farm roads and side lines and county roads all the way up to Thornbury and to Beaver River on Georgian Bay.

I knew the way when I was a kid in the light or in the dark. I knew which road to turn, how far it would go and turn here at this farm, turn at the school house, turn at the graveyard, all the way up to Thornbury and back.

Just as memorable, but certainly not so happy, was getting picked on in school

# Shawn Brush

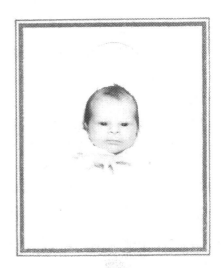

**Our Baby**

Name _SHAWN MICHAEL DAVID_

Born at _JOSEPH BRANT_

On _SATURDAY OCT. 11, 1969_

Time _10:48 P.M._

Weight _7 LB. 5 OZ._

Parents _MIKE & CARRY_

_BRUSH_

Shawn's baby book

by other kids because I was different. Kids can be cruel. Bullying is a major problem in our schools today - and over the silliest of reasons. It's not just the little kids, either, it is the big kids, too.

You can almost understand why grade school little ones make fun of people who are different, they just don't know any different. But there should be no excuses for those who are 8, 9, 10 years old who tease those who look different, dress differently, speak differently or act differently.

I was getting picked on pretty badly, especially by a set of twin brothers. One brother was causing me a lot of grief so my dad showed me how to defend myself with some boxing moves.

I bided my time and the next time he came after me, on the way back to school one lunch hour, I beat the snot out of him. I never got bothered again. Now, that's not what we are supposed to do – everyone tells us to turn the other cheek. But they are usually the ones who haven't faced this kind of treatment. Fighting back worked for me. It seemed to put an end to it. And, if others in the school had any ideas of taking me on because I was small and they thought I would be easy prey, they now had a different respect for this little guy who was different.

# The Krooked Cowboy

After the fight, I got called into the principal's office.

Around the same time I broke four bones in my ankle and foot, wrestling. My bones were brittle and breaks happened to me when other kids might have got away with a bruise,

The first day of Grade 4 I broke my left leg when I crashed my bicycle,

BRUSH — Mike and Mary Brush of 1091 Upper Sherman, Hamilton wish to announce the birth of Shawn Michael David weighing 7 lbs. 5 oz. at Joseph Brant Memorial Hospital at 10:49 p.m. on Saturday, October 11, 1969.

Proud parents announce Shawn's arrival

Grade 5 was when I started the operations for straightening my right leg. All those operations always took place in February, two years apart, so in Grade 5, Grade 7 and Grade 9 I missed a lot of school, although a few weeks after each operation I was back in class on crutches.

My grade school education was at St. Gabriel's Catholic school in Burlington. I was born and raised Catholic and church was next door to the school so there was all that stuff of baptism and communion.

Kindergarten to Grade 5 there are two floors to the school. Younger grades were on the ground floor, so the beginning of Grade 6 was up on the second floor with the older kids.

There were no elevators in the school. It was built at a time when everyone figured that it would be good exercise for elementary school kids to walk the stairs. After all, it wasn't too long before those who were designing the school were those who used to walk five miles to school every day through knee-deep snow, uphill both ways.

Shawn's first beer

I failed Grade 2. I am not proud of that, but I can't tell you why, either.

I used crutches at times to get around and help me up the stairs, but after the

23

# Shawn Brush

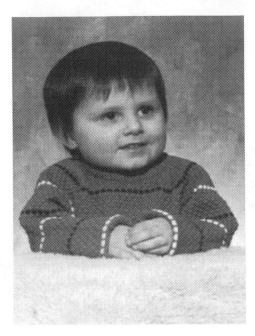

Not the traditional bearskin rug photo - thanks Mom and Dad!

operation in Grade 7, I had my first wheelchair.

I had some good friends at school because every time I needed to go up and down the stairs somebody had to carry the wheelchair – and had to carry me.

I have always tried to be independent. Even from an early age. If I had to wait for people to do things for me I would have wasted a lot of time. A lot of people helped me and I am appreciative of that. But can you imagine needing help with almost everything you do and every time you do them? It wasn't a matter of learning how to do something and not needing any help after a while when you got it right. No matter how many times I did things it always took me longer than the average kid.

So often at school I would sit on the floor and go up the stairs backwards, one step at a time. I would sit backwards on the step and, starting on the bottom step, push myself up with my hands as somebody carried up the chair. I was pretty physical and proud. I wanted to do it myself.

During recess I would stay in because it would be just too much to go up and down the stairs six times a day with the wheelchair.

So a kid has to have fun. And believe me, I just didn't sit sulking, or studying in the classroom, while the rest of the kids were out playing in the schoolyard.

The school was square, so I could go right around the top floor of the school, through the library and down both hallways. I was able to zip around the hallways very quickly. And I would do several laps every recess.

I also got pretty good at popping wheelies in the wheelchair and even being able to stay on two wheels for a long time, balancing myself. In fact, I could go all around the top floor of the school on two wheels.

Some of the other kids wanted to try popping wheelies, so I would jump

# The Krooked Cowboy

1975 at St. Gabriel's . . . Shawn is seated on the right.

1976 at St. Gabriel's . . . and Shawn is in his favourite seat.

out of the wheelchair and some kids would try to get it on two wheels right away. They were never patient enough to get the feel of it. If this little kid, Shawn, could do it then it must be a cinch. Hey, they soon found out that it wasn't all that easy.

25

# Shawn Brush

A trip to Fantasy Island, near Buffalo . . . and I was Davy Crockett.

# The Krooked Cowboy

1978 at St. Gabriel's . . . and Shawn switched his spot on the bench . . . he is on the left.

They would flip over in seconds. Everyone used to wipe out.

It wasn't much of a contest, although the kids looked at it that way. However, I had the most practice. So I always did the best.

I healed that summer and learned how to walk again. I remember I carved a couple of canes that spring when I went fishing at Thornbury. I got some vines that were growing along the Beaver River and pulled them up by the root, and cut them off to the right length and made the root the handle. I used them all that summer while I needed them during recovery.

When you think of kids in Grade 8 you think of healthy, inquisitive kids with minds of their own and boundless energy, just stepping out into the world of young adulthood as a first-year teenager.

As I entered my teens I was far from healthy and my energy level was low at best. To be honest with you, I couldn't even walk to the bus stop.

Going into Grade 8 I was taking a cab to school regularly.

We had moved further away from the school, and it was too much for me to even take a city bus.

27

# Shawn Brush

I used to enjoy the Cubs and Boy Scouts . . . I had so many good friends in uniform.

# The Krooked Cowboy

1977 , , , at St. Gabriel's . . . and Shawn is again seated at the right,

For me, this is when the music began because that's when I was taking a cab all the time and the cab driver Dan Robichaud was the person who taught me how to play guitar. Several years later I was able to repay him for all the time he spent with me when I was able to produce a cassette recording for him.

In the fall I went deer hunting and moose hunting with my dad. The reason I remember this in Grade 8 is because we went moose hunting in the last week of October. It was Halloween when we came back. It was snowing on the moose hunt and if we had stayed another few days we would have been snowed in.

We got home on Halloween and for some reason I was convinced that Nov. 1, All Saints Day, was a school holiday. I convinced my parents that there was no school. It was a nice day when I got home so I decided to go for a bike ride.

I was going by the school and to my surprise the school was open and, wouldn't you know it, the principal saw me riding my bike and he yelled, "Where are you going?"

I said, "Well, I am just going for a bike ride."

"Aren't you supposed to be in school?"

"Isn't it a day off?"

Helping the photographer on yearbook photo day at St. Gabriel's.

Happy Days with dad in the bush.

1948

1998

My mother's parents - Bert and Anne Van der Sanden from Welland, Ontario, who celebrated their 60th anniversary in 2008.

## 3
<hr>

# What a way to start Grade 4

I was in Grade 4 and I broke my left leg the first day of school, summer just ended.

I had a red bike with a cross beam like an old radio flyer style. It had funky handlebars.

I was sitting on it in the parking lot when a kid asked me if she could have a ride.

You know what kids are like. You have to have one last ride and then you can have a go.

I was no different. "I'm gonna go down there and do a stunt and then you can try it."

It was fine dust with gravel and then a grass lawn and a plaza behind it. I was going to spin the bike around. I did it okay, but when I put my foot down, the bike slid out from under me. I was doing the splits.

Martin O'Toole, a teenager in the townhouses came over and helped me up. His sister Anita babysat me when I was a kid. Everybody knew everybody in the townhouse complex. Martin was holding me up and saying I just had a charley horse.

## Shawn Brush

I was screaming.

His sister showed up and took me to apartment Number 3 where I lived.

My dad showed up and picked me up and I screamed even louder.

He took me to the hospital and they cut off my pants with scissors and did x-rays. The leg was broken. My mom showed up and the ambulance took me to the Hospital for Sick Children in Toronto where they knew me from previous visits.

I was put in traction and they wondered if they should operate. They usually don't allow children in hospital rooms, but one youngster came in and knocked into the traction and I screamed.

I'd still like to hit that kid. Funny thing is I'd be dreaming while I was lying prone. I'd go to take a step and I'd miss it and wake up because the muscles were flinching.

I loved riding my bike - and doing stunts. All kids love to have a bicycle and pop wheelies, skid the back tire. I learned a lot from my neighbour Doug Stewart. He lived two doors down with his sister and his mom. His mom worked in the drug store in Mount Royal Plaza. Doug was a couple of years older than me and we used to go and see movies. We went to see Steve Martin in *The Jerk*. He was kind of like my babysitter. He was an athlete. He was a cross-country runner and did the high jump.

One time, I remember, we were on the front yard and all the kids lay down for Doug who was going to long jump over us. Kind of like Evel Knievel of track and field.

I was the first kid in the line of friends he was jumping over. I don't remember much, except he kicked me in the eye and gave me a black eye. An accident, of course. Thank heavens he wasn't trying to do this on his bike.

# 4

# Squeaking through high school

Igraduated from high school, but they were far from the best years of my life.

It was nothing to do with the school, the teachers or my high school friends. When I look back at the school yearbook, Assumption Roman Catholic School in Burlington was a busy place.

Unfortunately, my condition had me lined up for a major operation in Grade 9. When you miss more than half of the school year, then are in a special Grade 10 class, it doesn't make for an auspicious start to high school.

I was popular in high school, among the students and the teachers, but that six weeks out of the classroom recovering from having my legs surgically broken put me so far behind that I did not recover academically.

I was different - and I stood out. Because of my size I couldn't even find clothes to fit me, never mind try to wear the school uniform – blue corduroy pants and a khaki or beige shirt. In my high school pictures you can see I am wearing clothes not even close to the school uniform.

Grade 9 started pretty normally, but when I went into hospital on Valentine's Day, everything changed for me.

# Shawn Brush

Grade 9 in 1985.

Grade 12 in 1988.

I attended classes every day before then, and even got involved in an art project helping to do a large mural at the school. After the operation I was in a cast and I couldn't reach to paint. I never touched it again.

The operation was not a surprise for me. I had the same procedure done in Grade 5 and Grade 7, so I knew what to expect. Each time I had what is called an osteotomy, an operation planned a few years earlier to take place during those three school grades.

# The Krooked Cowboy

Grade 10 in 1986.

The only difference in Grade 9 was that they were going to do both legs at the same time.

The surgery on my right leg was to straighten it. I was not bow-legged, I am ox-legged - the thigh being straight and the lower leg, the shinbone going out to your right or to your left.

When the leg is straightened they have to straighten the ankle. So although they straightened my leg so it was in line with my body I could not lock my right knee and I have never been able to lock it since. The result is my right leg doesn't fully extend, Both my arms are like that as well. I don't straighten my arms the whole way, so it is never fully straight, it is always bent.

It is not uncomfortable, but the right leg, of course, being shorter because I can't extend it, does cause some tiredness and wear and tear on my back and my hip joints, as well as other parts of the body that just don't perform as they are meant to move as they compensate for the way the rest of the body is operating.

# Shawn Brush

I went for therapy to try to get it straightened, but it never went straight again. Now let me explain the right kneecap. Visualize this . . . looking down your right knee, or if you look at it extended out in front of you, on the lower side - the shin side - there is muscle that runs straight down, pulls the kneecap and keeps it in place.

Now on the top there are two muscles, one on your outer thigh and one on your inner thigh. They pull the kneecap right and left from the top to keep it centred.

When I got out of that operation and out of the cast, my leg wouldn't straighten any more at the kneecap. It also pulled to one side, out to the outer side with the muscle on the top pulling it to the right on the right kneecap. The inner muscle was not responding any more and that was part of the therapy to try to get that muscle working. It still pulls to the right, so it never came back. There was no explanation why it never did.

It's popped out of place a couple of times. It just stopped doing it after a certain point, so it kind of corrected itself, although it still pulls to the right.

Grade 9 was when I had both legs done simultaneously. Allow me to describe the procedure a bit more because what they do is straighten the leg like you have the two bones that you see on a skeleton or an X-ray in your shin. They cut into the tibia and cut out an angle to straighten the leg to where it would be in the best position. I have a scar down the front of the shin and another down the calf muscle on both legs in a similar position.

The scars are about five inches long and there is a piece of metal in there in the front and in the back. It looks like a giant staple that goes in either bone and aligns it, keeping it in place during the procedure and then it is left in there.

They go in, they saw and cut and move the bone, take out the bone, place the bone where they want it put in these giant staples that are about as long as the incision. I remember seeing them and I can still feel them in my legs.

Then they sew you up and put you in a cast.

It is not pleasant. No fun at all, actually. It is painful like you wouldn't believe and when it's all done it is debateable whether you are any better off. I realise that there is no cure for what I have. The operations are to perhaps give me a little better flexibility and mobility now and in the future.

It's supposed to be short term pain for long term gain. In my case, I have to say the pain has not warranted the gain - at least for me. Now I am not sure whether my suffering has helped any other child suffering from a similar disease.

Because there is no cure, you go through these operations probably more so to help the doctors study your body's reaction to the treatment so that those that follow may benefit. When you think about it the medical profession is all about trial and error and experimentation. How would you ever find ways to make patients and sufferers more comfortable, if those going before were not willing to take the chances of improving their own lifestyle?

My mother and father made the decision for me to go through these operations in Grades 5, 7 and 9. Doctors wanted to carry on and do more of these operations as I got into adulthood, but I decided I had enough. As I look back I have convinced myself that I would not have benefitted from further operations.

I have often thought whether I was selfish in not permitting the doctors to do more procedures on my body. But I soon remember all that pain and feel that most mortals faced with my situation would make a similar decision.

I still have dreams about those operations – and they took place more than 20 years ago.

In one, I am walking up a set of stairs, thinking there is one more step - but there isn't, I go to step up one last step it is not there, and I jar my leg and stumble forward.

Another dream takes me back to when I had broken my leg and others, of course, during operations when your muscles twitch and you are kind of screaming.

This is not something I can glide through and it is certainly not the most pleasant of memories for the most part.

I have mixed feelings.

The people who love you, your mom and dad, and the people who want to help you are convinced – or at least have faith – that this operation is going to help you and make you stronger and better. Problem is, I am the one having to go through all this pain.

It kind of plays a funny thing on you if you let it. Here's the good guy in a white coat who is the doctor, who like a policeman or a fireman are people who you are supposed to trust.

They cut you open and break your leg and move it to a different place, put a big piece of metal in it, sew you up and put you in a cast. Two months later, you come back and let them do it again and two years later they are going to do it to you again, and then another two years after that, again all the pain.

So it doesn't leave a very good taste in your mouth.

I remember being in the hospital, well back to my childhood, sleeping.

I always slept in the morning and my dad would get me up and say "come on it is time for school."

I would wake up, and I would physically feel I was up, get out of bed and get dressed and go downstairs to get my breakfast. My dad would be standing in the kitchen saying "come on, it's time to go" and I would wake up and I would be back in bed, like astral projection. I would be thinking 'why are you yelling, I am right here?'

That happened quite a bit when I was in the hospital, all doped up.

A hypnotist friend of mine, said to me a few years ago, that some of these things that happened to me occur when you are in pain so you leave any way you can. That produces an out of body experience. I have had a few of these types of dreams in my life, some in the hospital. They were very realistic, or felt like out of body experiences, or however anybody wants to interpret them, supernatural or otherwise.

One I remember vividly has me floating around the halls of the hospital. Interestingly enough, it is not that I am walking at my height when that would happen, (or does happen, because I am not ruling out that it will again happen in my life). It is more like eye-level with the upper limits of the room or the view of where I am flying or floating, that's common with astral projection which I read about later in my teens and early twenties. I studied it a little bit because it was something that continued for a little while. It hasn't happened for a long time.

I remember waking up in the recovery room in the hospital after the Grade 9 operation. It is not a place that you consciously remember because you come out of the operating room and that is where they take you to stabilize you.

Now, as I remember, along one wall there are some windows and your head is to the wall with the bed against that side. Opposite the wall was a walkway where the nurses and doctors would wheel in the beds with patients from the operating room.

I woke up and the only way I can describe it is like a war zone . . . a triage kind of thing where there is a nurse and a whole bunch of patients. They are all knocked out, of course, and the thing that is odd about it is it feels like you are watching a movie and floating up high, so I was looking down on all this.

I can see the nurse and a couple of other people and there is this one person, or kid and he is screaming. He is in a lot of pain and I am saying to the nurse, trying to say to the nurse, that this person needs help and I can't help them for some reason.

I continue to try to get the nurse's attention, but the screaming goes on. They are in a lot of pain. They are in agony and I am trying to get the attention of the nurse and I am getting madder and madder because she is not hearing me. Finally, I have to start yelling at her and try to grab her arm to get her attention and the next thing I know I wake up and I am in the bed and it is me screaming.

It only lasts for a little while. It is not something I can remember consciously. It is like watching a movie, very surreal.

They give me a shot of a drug, a painkiller, and I black out and I don't come to again until the next time I am ready for more painkiller.

Those moments – and there are others that are similar – are very vivid. What was explained to me is that I had come out of the operating room and had not had the painkiller yet, so I had fully felt that intensity without any relief. Like I was waking up and experiencing that pain, and that intensity, without a buffer zone, without any relief.

So that one was pretty traumatic. Then, of course, having to go back two months later and have the lower side done, you probably understand my reluctance to want to continue with these operations into adulthood.

The lower side was less intense because there were no pins and it was a very small incision.

In my medical record I think it says they wanted to do it again when I was 16 and I just flat out told them "No way."

I don't think I have been any worse for wear for not having had that procedure done at 16.

Some other things about that darkness that consumes you and the pain and the drugs and stuff. You don't eat when you go in for an operation and then you don't eat for a couple of days. You are eating jello and soup, so you become very weak.

You wake up and you are in pain and someone comes along and sticks a needle in you and you just go black. Your eyes just fade into this black and then you wake up with one of those dreams where you are walking down the street and you go to step off the curb, but there is no curb. You wake up, your muscles flinch, you scream, nurse comes along and sticks a needle in you.

My doctor at Sick Kids was  probably one of the leading guys in the world in his field of medicine.  But I always thought the kid next to me in the room was getting better attention.

Let me explain. Maybe the kid had a broken leg. His doctor would check up with him and maybe say something like, 'Okay, everything seems to be in order, blah! Blah! Blah! The doctor would go away.

When my doctor came to see me he would come in with four or five other doctors. They would talk among themselves, either 'this is what we are going to do,' or 'this is what we did.' Trailing along behind them would be 15 or 20 medical students and oddly enough I don't ever remember anyone there for my mind, so to speak.

All these doctors were coming to see me, but not one was there for my mind. They were not really coming to see me, they were coming to see the work they had done.

After the Grade 9 operation my friend Dave MacLean didn't know whether I was going to be able to play guitar with the two casts on. He had brought along a fiddle, thinking that I could keep up the playing and do something.

When he walked in I was sitting on the floor with both legs stretched out in front of me with a pillow against my back, kind of leaning back, watching TV and I had the guitar across my stomach and chest and I was playing. It didn't deter me at all. I found a way to do it. Just kept up the playing, so I got my guitar lessons and just kept it up.

Looking back, it is too bad I didn't have the same determination for school work.

While bluegrass was my first love in the high school years,  I liked listening to Jimi Hendrix, and I acquired an electric guitar somewhere along the way. But the acoustic guitar was my instrument.

I was skipping classes regularly in Grade 10, partially because it was the cool thing to do and it was just too hard for me to walk across the field. I was either late or sore.

So I would sit in the cafeteria and play my guitar. I would sit in the smokers' pit and hang out with the cool kids and play some guitar.

# The Krooked Cowboy

We also had a chapel in our high school and you could go in there and play some music and have some quiet time. So I got to be part of the choir because that's where I hung out and played my guitar.

I was in a couple of special classes - even in grade school days - for helping me to catch up on my studies because I had missed some classes because of the operations.

I had missed a couple of weeks here and a couple of weeks there and didn't really realise I had a problem until I got to college and there I had to take a special grammar course because my grammar wasn't very good for reading and writing.

I remember in my high school English class they said I had a very good understanding. My verbal skills were excellent as was my comprehension of poetry.

I put this down to one of the things back in my childhood on all those trips going fishing with my dad when he would recite Robert Service poems like *Dangerous Dan McGrew* and *The Cremation of Sam McGee*. I have a couple of those books from when I was a kid along with my Boy Scout uniforms and things like that.

I guess I got an early appreciation for oral storytelling, good poetry. I could recite them at the drop of a hat at one point.

I would struggle a little bit now, but could do it, I think.

Grade 10 I did a lot of sitting in the smokers' pit playing guitar. Some of the teachers said, 'bring your guitar to class' because I would actually go to class if I could bring the guitar. They would ask me to play a tune and being in special classes for people with learning disabilities - or people who needed extra help I was able to do that regularly. By that I mean there was not the pressure in those special classes to learn the prescribed math theory in this 45 minute class, or it may put the program behind schedule. My peers and I were there in class, that was important.

The other thing that started between Grade 9 and Grade 10 was I went to my first bluegrass jam session and before long I was attending these events all around the area five or six nights a week.

In Grade 10, I was the only student in a tutoring class to help me keep up with my studies. Just me and the teacher. I just looked at her one day and said, 'I don't really need to be in here' and made it a point that I was not getting any help in there. Somehow, I had hurt her feelings in the process and I ended up having a spare class for the remainder of the year because it was too late to get into another class.

That open period was supposed to be my study period. I was still skipping classes and the logic I never understood at high school was that if you missed a class you had a detention and if you missed a detention you would get another detention. Then if you missed the two detentions you got a day off.

So I didn't figure they had things thought out very well because I was getting exactly what I wanted. I would get suspended for a day or three days.

Finally, it ended with an agreement with the principal who said, 'If you don't want to go to class, just come to tell me where you are. Don't leave the property.'

So that was the deal. So I would go to the principal and say, "You know what, I don't feel like going to math today. I will be in the cafeteria, or I will be in the library." And he would say "fine" because he knew where I was. It wasn't as though I was out shoplifting, or smoking dope, or stealing something, or I was missing.

My grades were good enough that I was passing. So that was acceptable for all parties, including me. I later had a saying when I referred to musicians, that 'good is good, but great is better.' I suppose things could have been a lot different if I had applied that to myself and my school work. I was 'good enough' to graduate from each year's high school and that was without attending many classes.

I was right back in the swing of things in Grade 11, playing every night, skipping classes. I only failed a couple of things. I know math was one. Maybe one or two other things I failed, but not much considering how much I missed. I just squeaked by.

While I was skipping classes I remember at lunch hour most days I would leave with my buddy Roger and drive up to the farm to ride the motorcycle or the snowmobile for an hour, get back in the truck and go back to school, to skip more classes.

My days were full.

I was 19 when I got my Grade 12 at M.M. Robinson High School in Burlington. I needed three credits to graduate so I took piano, physics and math. All three were first thing in the morning, so then my days were free.

I enjoyed the piano course, which has helped me later in life with my music.

# The Krooked Cowboy

Other than this course I never had any formal music training, except for trumpet in Grade 9 and a guitar course later in high school.

I did all right in the Grade 12 courses and I graduated, but I didn't go to the graduation ceremonies at either high school. Neither did I go to any prom. I was just so glad that the high school years were over.

Shawn after winning a bluegrass songwriting award in Ontario in the early 90s.

# Shawn Brush

Shawn with a young fan, Aaron Urquhardt, of Hamilton.

# 5

# Cabs and copying

My Grade 12 friends had part-time jobs, or were looking for summer jobs. I was 17 and a couple of credits short of graduating from high school.

I was happy doing my own thing but then I found out Burlington Taxi, the cab company that drove me to school, was looking for a dispatcher so they could go on vacation in the summer. They were willing to train somebody. I couldn't drive cab but I could talk and sit at the desk.

Sitting in a cab every school day for five years you hear all the radio babble, and I have pretty good auditory skills, so after school instead of going home I went to the Burlington Taxi office. I got the job.

I remember the lady who trained me smoked Benson and Hedges 100s and drank tea like it was going out of style.

She was training me to be a dispatcher. She had a map on the wall and they have so many cars out at one time.

It was like playing chess because you had to know who everybody was – and where they were - at any given time.

You had to give the ride to the right person. If someone was at the Burlington Mall sitting waiting you knew his cab was available.

There were all kinds of little political things you had to be aware of, like not playing favourites and being smart businesswise because you could send a person half-way across town if you were not careful.

Like everything else, I suppose, you can get people mad at you fairly quickly – customers and drivers. Some days you would have a good day because that's the way the luck would run. Some days it would be awful. It seemed everyone had a short fuse and it didn't take long for them to get upset – customers thinking they were waiting too long, or drivers not having a fare for the past half-hour.

It was a pretty good education for a 17-year-old kid, but it was the beginning of summer and all my friends had good jobs and they were planning on going to the beach every weekend and going to Belleville and to provincial parks and beaches on weekends. My friends wanted me to go with them to the beach, but the taxi company owners decided they only wanted me to work on weekends. I didn't like the thought of just working the weekends. If that was the case I wasn't going to make very much money.

They were training me every day and that's when I found out I was eligible for this disability pension with the Ontario Government, through the welfare system, which is now called ODSP (Ontario Disability Support Program), part of Family and Social Services.

It was under the Family Benefits Act at that time. I was eligible for it because of my disability and because I couldn't go to work at many places – even at some of the prime spots taken by students – fast food restaurants and gas stations. Theoretically, I could go and do things in these places, but I couldn't reach the fryer, things like that. It was the height restrictions primarily that prevented me from working in places where my peers found work. I suppose it was a safety issue, too. Again, this could be put down primarily to my height, but reaching up for things like the fryer could be hazardous for me, and my fellow staff members.

The cab dispatching job looked like a real feasible thing, but it was best I quit because I didn't want to do just the weekend shifts.

There was also a maturity issue because I was dealing with people twice my age and I really had to be on the ball. I am not saying I couldn't handle it, but I just don't think I was ready for it.

Part of my job though when I was being trained as a dispatcher was I had to go and get tea and cigarettes for the trainer, who was a dispatcher.

So I quit the dispatcher job because I wanted to have summer weekends off to

# The Krooked Cowboy

hang out with my friends.

Fred Robson had worked in a place in Oakville called BCP (Blast Cleaning Products) and they were looking for somebody to take a summer job.

I guess they also needed to hire somebody who was physically disabled because they were a big company and they needed that just to look good.

So I went in for an interview at BCP, an American-owned company. They built sand-blasting painting machines all in one for locomotives and box cars, mostly for box cars.

For example, CP Rail wants to paint a box car, it goes through this piece of equipment and it sandblasts it and paints it.

BCP made these machines from concept through to finished fabrication and they ship them all over.

What they had were blueprinters, draughters, engineers and welders all on staff and working in-house and they needed me to update and file away everything. The drawings were as big as me - about two feet wide and four feet long - and they would hang on a rack in a hanging file. They had anywhere from 200 to 300-plus drawings that were old and worn out. They would need to be filed in a room with large drawers and numbered for easy access.

Fred was the one who suggested me for the job. About four doors from where I lived was a family named the Thibodeaus. Sharon Thibodeau worked at BCP and she drove in every morning at 7 a.m. That's when they wanted me to start, so I had a ride to work right from my front door every day and home again.

I worked all summer.

My job was basically to just do the hanging files, but I also had to do a lot of retrieval work. I ended up doing two jobs.

Fall came around and I didn't want to go to school for a whole year for just two or three credits so I ended up working until November. It was kind of tough on me that job because I was working with adults, there was no one my age.

Once the bosses' daughter was away at school, there was no one under 30 working there.

I would see the guys and I would go to Buffalo drinking with one of my friends.

Several weekends I went with my friends to Belleville.

# Shawn Brush

Through the week I would get up early and go to work and sleep on my breaks. Not because I was staying out late, but because it was a very physical job for me. There was a lot of climbing up and down a ladder, getting in the file drawer and carrying the files. Now pieces of paper are not that heavy, but 20 or 30 the size of your whole body and it all adds up.

At 4 o'clock I would get home and I would just collapse.

When I did that job with the blast cleaning products I started to realise that I can't do this and I should go back to school and start thinking about doing some other things.

I gave them my notice. It was kind of a funny way I left that job.

Every once in a while at BCP I would lay down on the table and have a break. The coffee truck would come and I would go and grab a sandwich on break and I had a walkman on whenever I was working and I would have Guns 'N' Roses on and Metallica. Funny music choices, I'll agree, for a bluegrass guy like me. I got into trouble for walking around in the office with Guns 'N' Roses playing so loud . . . and me singing away.

One time I was in the file room laying down on the table.

I was out gallivanting the night before, so I was listening to music and taking it easy . . . but getting the job done. I had stopped to have a break and was lying down on the table and was almost asleep and the boss of our department came in. He had a group of Japanese businessmen he was taking on tour of the plant.

Of course, that didn't go over too well.

I went to give my notice and I knew from experience that they had trouble finding someone, or keeping someone that was good, so I gave them a lot of notice. The next day a fellow who was in charge of that division called me into his office.

I had been there nearly six months and I had never seen the inside of this guy's office, so I knew something was up. He said. "Well, you gave us your notice, why don't you leave on Friday?"

This was a Tuesday or Wednesday, "Oh, is that the way it is?"

I was trying to be cool about it and say, "I hope you are going to be able to find someone."

It was about 10 in the morning, so I said "Why don't I leave right now?"

# The Krooked Cowboy

And I did.

I walked out of there and said send my holiday cheque. I got a taxi and came home and I never looked back.

Shawn with one of the many prizes from his moose hunting trips.

**6**

---

# Go-kart crash smashes knee

I went go-karting one day with a few friends. We were out on the beach strip in Hamilton having fun.

I crashed the go-kart into the wall and I hit my knee against the steering wheel.

Dave Rusnell and another guy came over and asked if I was okay.

"Yeah, yeah," and I drove around another couple of times.

I had hit my knee on the inside sideways.

When I got out I could hardly walk.

Alita said, "Are you okay?"

"Yeah. Yeah. I just bruised it."

We went back to Alita's townhouse.

My knee had swelled up and my jeans were tight. She put some ice on it.

I got up to go to the washroom and I fell right on my face. I couldn't bend my leg and I couldn't straighten it.

Alita said, "That's it. I am taking you to the hospital."

## Shawn Brush

I said, "Oh it's okay. It's just bruised. It will be alright in the morning and in a couple of weeks it will go away."

My pain threshold is pretty high, but she seemed to know that something more serious had happened to me than a bruising.

She insisted on taking me to the hospital and that was the end of that.

We went down to the hospital. It had happened in the afternoon and it was suppertime now. It was busy in the emergency department and 9 o'clock rolled around before it was my turn to see the doctor.

The nurse wanted me to go and get some x-rays of the knee. Now, if you have ever had a broken bone you know that if you move it - no matter which way – it hurts like hell.

This nurse said she had to take a picture of my knee and they had to do it in layers so they can see any bone chips within the joint. So she takes one x-ray, moves the knee to get the next angle.

They had to take 15 x-rays.

She was pushing my knee and she asks, "Can you bend your leg?" So I bend my leg.

It took a long time. She went to get all the x-rays developed.

When she came back she had tears in her eyes. She was crying.

I said, "It's broken, isn't it?

She just hugged me and she said "I'm sorry."

I said again, "It's broken, eh?"

And she said, "I can't tell you. You have to see the doctor."

Again, I said, "It's broken, right?"

She had tears in her eyes. She realised how much pain she had put me through.

I went back and waited for a doctor and about midnight or one o'clock he comes in and tells me I will have to go home and come back to the hospital in the morning.

"We have to get a specialist because I don't know how to handle this because of the bone condition and the break." He gave me some pills for the pain and he gave me some crutches.

# The Krooked Cowboy

I had been used to getting the run-around from doctors all my life. I suppose when you consider that I am a rarity - in that only one in half a million have my condition – that most doctors don't get to see anyone like me in their entire career.

I understand why they send you from one doctor to the another, but as the patient it becomes very taxing on the nerves and on your patience when doctor after doctor can't help you.

As a kid you finally get to Toronto's Hospital for Sick Children, one of the best in the world. That's where I was diagnosed as a youngster and had been treated there for more than 15 years as I was growing up.

So, my friends drive me home. Mom and Dad were sleeping. Alita wants to make sure I get to my bedroom upstairs. There's a lot of noise and my mom and dad wake up.

"What's going on?"

"I broke my knee."

"What?"

"I have to go back in the morning."

So at 8 in the morning I go back down to the hospital and the doctor comes in. He was a really good doctor. He says you have broken your tibia plateau and that is just like it sounds, a plate, a small thin bone. It is in between your knee and your femur, behind the kneecap. Usually athletes break it from shock, from a blow. Football players run into this type of injury when they get tackled.

Whenever you break a joint the blood swells up and clots the joint to keep everything immobile to protect it until it gets the proper treatment. It is Mother Nature's way of keeping everything in place.

If you shatter it they have to go in there surgically and piece everything together.

Luckily I had broken it in such a way that the plate had just cracked in two. It didn't move up or down or sideways or diagonally, so there was no surgery needed. As long I stayed off it and protected it I was going to be okay.

He looked at me and looked at my charts. It was summer time and he said to me, "You have broken a bone before?" "Yeah."

"Do you want a cast?"

"Not really."

"If I wrap it in a bandage you have to be really careful and you have to stay off it."

Great. I don't need a cast and now I can still go swimming. I just have to take it easy.

He gave me a bunch of pills for pain and wrapped it up in a bandage and said rewrap it every day.

"If you go swimming just be careful. Don't put any weight on it and come back and see me in six weeks."

That summer I went to the cottage in Bear Creek. My sister rented it one time and my mother rented it later, so I basically went up there for a month. I just sat on the beach drinking beer and walking around when I felt good.

I walked into the doctor's office about five weeks later and he said, "You are not supposed to be walking on it."

He x-rayed it and said it had healed, however, my right knee still doesn't straighten.

Shawn in concert.

# Shawn Brush

Dave Brown photo

This is the only photograph of Shawn playing at Humber College.

## 7

# Off to college

I got accepted into the radio broadcasting program at Humber College in Etobicoke. I didn't drive so I had no way of getting there. My friend Dave Brown got accepted for audio-visual and production. He didn't know how he was getting there either. School was about to start and I was walking with my cane and just getting going again. My knee had healed from a go-kart accident.

Dave's grandpa gave him a car, made in 1964, and Dave put up a sign on the college bulletin board for anyone who wanted to carpool. A girl I knew from grade school and high school wanted to ride with us. And there was a guy from Oakville, who was also taking radio, who needed a ride in. The car turned out to be a typical student car, serving all of us. In the very first month of school we discovered a hole in the trunk. This meant we had to drive with the windows open or we would have been overcome by carbon monoxide poisoning. It was September. Having the windows open was not much of a problem, except on rainy days.

Winter was another story. There was no way we would be able to use this car come winter. Not unless the hole was fixed and that wasn't likely to happen. It was expensive on gas, too. We realised pretty quickly that we were not going to be able to drive that car. Dave had no money. I only had a little bit saved.

Dave's parents and I came up with a solution. We bought a car together to take us all to school. I put in the money to buy my half of the car and that would be my gas for the year, or for however long the car lasted.

It was a piece of junk car, a Toyota, but it did the job. In fact, Dave got a job delivering pizzas so the car was used every minute of every hour of the day. School 'bus' in the day and pizza delivery 'truck' by night. Eventually that schedule was too much for the Toyota and it died.

But while it was still running we got up at 5:30 every morning. I would call Dave, giving him his regular wakeup call. Then we would pick up Diana and on to Oakville to pick up Scott.

Scott was pretty young. He was 17 or 18 at the time and already going to college. Scott spent his early teen years in Germany and it was there he learned to play drums. He is a good drummer. Today he works in a music store in Oakville. Scott proved to be another one of my musical friends.

Just as we were all getting into college life there was a teachers' strike in November. It lasted about a month. Dave and I had nothing to do. He was working part-time doing the pizza thing. I had a little bit of money saved so we decided to go fishing. We packed up the car in the middle of November and drove up to Georgian Bay. We checked into the hotel, stayed up there for a few days and went fishing. Dave was more interested in fishing. I was just happy to get away and have a good time. We did. Little did I know, it was one of many adventures to come.

There was another kid in the radio program who was a big country fan and he knew I liked bluegrass.

He was a fan of Don Williams and we liked a lot of the same music, including Waylon Jennings and others. Ian Tyson was playing in Toronto and he asked me if I wanted to go to see him. Now at this time I still didn't think I would go and play music for a living.

So I went with my friend to see Ian and Sylvia Tyson and I was sure glad I did. We wanted to go early because it was in a big bar and we wanted a good seat. When we got there people were already lined up. We sat at a table right front dead centre. The band was having supper beside us. Tom Russell came out and opened the show and he alone was worth the price of admission and the effort to get there. I was blown away by this guy. I thought he was more entertaining and had better songs than Ian and Sylvia but I had never heard of him. Then Sylvia Tyson came out, and then Ian Tyson. What a great night. Little did I know it would change my life. I didn't get home that night until 3 or 4 in the morning, so I took the next day off of school. That was something else I did when going to college.

Humber had a pretty big campus and I just can't do a lot of walking. They had a cafeteria and a student bar. Problem was, the student bar was way at the other end of the school. The cafeteria was in the middle of the grounds. The teachers' lounge, which served alcohol, was right where most of my classes were and where my locker was. It was close by. We parked at that end of the building.

As I mentioned, that fall I took a grammar test and found out that I had to take an English course. All the time I had missed at school during months of operations had left me deficient in English. I was in a course that would suit my voice – working in radio - but of course a certain proficiency in English is expected. And rightly so. Voice classes and reading out loud were to help us work on our professional speaking voice. Coincidentally, some of the same techniques are used when teaching singing. Working in a radio studio, recording jingles gave us a good look at the technical side and creatively we were writing jingles for advertising and also writing news stories and reporting. There was also a sales class to show us the finer art of selling ads. I also had that English grammar class to squeeze in.

What struck me about college was the different way of teaching. The professors were always dealing with a lot students and there is no favouritism, or at least there didn't appear to be. They treated everyone on the same level. It was an exhausting time because I was getting up early and the days were full. I would get in the car and sleep on the way to school and sleep on the way back.

Most days I would eat lunch in the teachers' lounge - and drink beer. I wasn't cozying up to any of them, it was just better for me to use the teachers' lounge during a break. I would never have been able to walk to the cafeteria and back to class. They had good deals and good food and all the domestic brands. Drank a lot of beers in those college years. My first year of college we were doing all of that stuff. Classes seemed to be going well and I was pleased with the course. I had some counsellors who would say to me "Why don't you take a computer class, Shawn? Why don't you take a typing class?"

# Shawn Brush

When I was in high school there was this underlying tone where people were trying to say things, without really saying it. I am a pretty blunt person, and live by the principle, 'Say what you mean, mean what you say.' I started to get a feeling coming from some of the college teachers.

They would talk to me about radio and say that it was a job where you have got to pay your dues. You have to work hard. Stay up all night. Go out into the field. And you have to do all kinds of jobs in the radio business before getting your own show. I thought most jobs you had to pay your dues, so to speak, before making your own mark. Here I was thinking I was doing fine in class, and above all enjoying it. I was thinking what a great job radio would be for me. Now, my teachers were asking me if I had thought about doing something else?

Anyhow, that's the message I was getting. Nobody would come out and say that - and that's what I mean by this underlying tone. I think they were just trying to be kind by asking if I had thought about taking a computer course, or maybe an accounting course. I would rather have not played the game.

I paid my money to be in the radio course and to eventually work in radio. I think it would have been much more professional on their part to say, "Hey, look Shawn, things are not working out the way we would like. It seems you have a problem with this, or that, or the other. Now have you thought about another career if this one doesn't work out?" Now something like that would have gotten my attention.

With a frank talk, I would have been better equipped to understand how I was really doing. I would have been thinking about wanting to save my radio hopes vs. switching to another program. With all this beating-around-the-bush talk you don't really know where you stand. Does he mean this? Should I do that? Am I failing? I think straight talk is so much more useful. It's fair too. After all, you don't want to spend time and money in a two or three year program only to find out when it comes to graduation time you are not going to graduate. Or you are, but just barely. Or you are never going to find work in the field of radio – just because you couldn't figure out the less-than-frank messages of your teachers a year or two earlier.

I think that these mixed messages from teachers started to take its toll on me. Also, my friends had grown up and they all had part-time jobs - and girlfriends. Many were living on their own. One of my friends was a policeman already. Another was in the army.

Here was me. Living at home with my parents. I didn't have a job. I had my little pension from the government. I continued on my path - playing my guitar, drinking beer and having fun. And I continued to go to school – in the radio program!

Dave Brown got upset one day at something on the radio and actually pulled the radio out of the car and threw it out onto the road on Ford Drive in Oakville. He physically pulled it right out of the dash because he was stressed out. And that was the end of the radio. Another morning we got into the car and he said, "Have you got any money?" I said, "No." He said he had already put gas in and we continued on to pick up the next person in our crew. Have you got any money? No. We went on to Oakville and continued on our way. Suddenly he announced we had no oil in the car. We travelled about 40 kilometres – just a few short of the college – and the engine started knocking and banging and smoking. We pulled over to the shoulder of the road. Yup, the engine had blown and seized up.

Dave got out and opened the hood up. No one stopped. Scott got out and tried to wave down a tow truck.

Still no one was stopping. Then I got out and stood on the side of the road for a minute. It was 7 a.m. in the morning. A van stopped and a woman came over. Dave said, "thanks for stopping." She said, "Oh, I recognized Shawn." Turns out, she knew me from seeing me around the college campus. I said I would stay with Dave and get the car towed. It was more of an adventure to stay with Dave, of course, than to sit in the classroom. Eventually, we got a tow truck and the guy towed us right down to the Lakeshore in Toronto.

The engine was a write-off but we still had a couple more months of school. Dave's mom and step-dad said they were already tapped out and they could not help us with any money for a replacement engine or another car. My folks couldn't help and I was broke. Luckily, Dave's biological dad, who lived in Seattle, had a friend who owned a car dealership. He arranged to get Dave a truck and before we knew it we were back on the road again and everything was good. We even had a radio in the truck!

One day I remember I came home exhausted. I hadn't played my guitar for a couple of weeks and I was writing out some homework, some commercials. I picked up my guitar and it felt good to play my guitar.

I started playing a little melody and words started to come to me.

I wrote them down. I wasn't thinking about writing a song consciously but through the process of being in the mind frame of reporting and writing jingles because we would write to time for a 30-second spot that you then had to read it in that time. There were only so many syllables a minute. You could look at your written material and tell that it was 30 seconds or 45 seconds or a minute. I could tell that I had a three-minute song with music and lyric.

With a little help from his friends . . . Shawn taught himself to play a number of instruments - including the banjo.

## 8

# Advertising jingles start new *Seasons* in my life

It was at college, learning to write advertising jingles when I discovered my love for songwriting.

I came up with this song, very naturally and without too much effort. It was *Seasons*.

It goes:

*In the Spring we are born never knowing any wrong*

*Our parents tell us to be strong and with the rain we are gone.*

After the spring we have summer, so I wrote about the summer. Then we have fall and then winter, of course.

I looked at it then and knew it needed a chorus.

I put in a chorus:

*Like the seasons we must change,*

*never, no never turning back, growing up, growing old, going fast,*

*like the seasons of the past.*

## Shawn Brush

I put a guitar break at the end.

Then sang the chorus and the bridge. Then I put it away.

I wrote *The Wooden Hill* in much the same way and sitting in the same spot.

This was in our house on Manchester Drive in Burlington. It was a semi split and you come in the front door and there was a long hallway to the kitchen with the living room on the right. A dining room at the back with a kitchen and the stairs to the second floor on the left.

I sat and did all my homework sitting in the living room, looking at the stairs. That's where I wrote *Seasons* and then I was sitting there one day and I thought about the *Wooden Hill*.

I didn't have the guitar in my hand.

I just thought the *Wooden Hill*...and it went like this:

*In our house there's a stairwell that I call the wooden hill*

It basically wrote itself, so to speak, I reached over and picked up the guitar and just spoke the words out loud. I found a chord that sounded good and it ended up being in the key of F and I put the capo on the guitar. A capo is a clamp that you put over the strings on the neck of the guitar to be able to play in different keys with basic chords. Then I just kind of followed my voice. I put the chords there, I had a melody there already and just followed my nose and had a song, very quickly, very simply and very easily.

Those two songs won me the bluegrass awards for central Canada.

But that came later on, of course, because I was still shy and didn't want to sing my songs.

I continued writing these songs in my spare time and it was just coming naturally. I was expressing myself - and I really hadn't done that before.

**9**

# Why, oh why, Wyoming?

When I got my first credit card I bought a pair of cowboy boots. They were too big for me, but I bought them anyway. They were cheap. And I just wanted to use the card. I also bought a cowboy hat.

That little card was marvellous. I was able to buy little things here and there. Stuff I really didn't need. My new-found freedom to spend money that I didn't have just meant I had joined the buy now and pay later society. And like so many before me, I wasn't able to control myself. I had this wonderful card and it was buying me lots of stuff.

I wasn't thinking about who was going to pay for it all – or when.

I wasn't working at the time and all that was important to me was that I was spending, spending, spending and did not have to pay any cash.

If I wanted to go someplace I had the power to do it by just putting gas in the car and going.

Labor Day weekend 1992 I went to a party, had a few beers and a couple of cigarettes, some joints that were flying around and I left that party at a farm west of Hamilton.

I knew I was in no shape to drive so I pulled over in Ancaster. I parked in the driveway of a couple of friends, Doug Juby and Jane McKenzie. I fell asleep in the car.

# Shawn Brush

Next morning Doug was up early making coffee and I was frustrated, wanting to do something. I felt that my life at that time was pointless and every direction I was taking wasn't leading me to anything I liked, or that was positive. There didn't seem to be a lot of open doors for me and I was so down that I didn't see anything bright on the horizon.

I ate and ran that morning. Just didn't feel like hanging around. That's unusual for me because it takes me a long time to get going each day, especially when I have had a late night partying.

This morning was different. I don't know why. Maybe I was just so frustrated with what I felt like, I said, "I gotta go."

Doug said, "Where are you going?

I said the first thing that came to my mind – "Wyoming."

He repeated what I said and made it a one word question, "Wyoming?"

"Yes, I'm going to the mountains."

Then he said, "Get me a souvenir."

And that was a challenge that I had to accept. I had no intention of going to Wyoming when I said "Wyoming." But now I was getting excited about the idea.

I was just going to get home, pack, run away and become a mountain man.

Well, that was a bit much. That wasn't ever going to happen. But I was going to go to Wyoming and I was going to get a souvenir for Doug. That comment was the clincher. Funny how little things can change your life.

I stopped at home long enough to throw some clothes in a suitcase. I wasn't in the best of shape because I'd partied all weekend.

I had a three day beard and I was pale. I hadn't eaten right.

But nothing was dissuading me from heading out for Wyoming. I jumped in the car and I started driving. I got to London, Ontario, pulled into the truck stop there and got something to eat at McDonald's.

I grabbed some snacks for the road and got back on the 401 heading down to Detroit. Well, I had only been driving a minute or two and was sipping my milkshake having a bite of the hamburger. I am barrelling down the fast lane because there's a whole bunch of cars in the slow lane and the highway is only two lanes wide. Way behind me I could see flashing lights on a cruiser. He's coming up fast. People are getting out of his way and so I'm looking for a spot to slip over to get out of his way but no-one is letting me in.

It's just bumper to bumper, so I speed up a little to get out of this guy's way. There wasn't a soft shoulder on the left, I would have had to take to the ditch in the middle of the highway and I didn't even consider it an option,

He's getting closer to me so I give it more gas and speed up a little bit more and I'm still looking for a spot to get over, but no one is giving way to let me in.

He's really flying behind me and the lights are flashing and I can see now it's an OPP cruiser, just as I had earlier suspected.

I give it even more gas and start speeding up even more to get out of his way because he's obviously after somebody. Finally, I see a spot to get over, but I'm going too fast now to get into the slower lane so my only option was to go a little faster.

Now I'm really going fast, and this cruiser's right behind me. Wow, he must be really after somebody.

It wasn't long after that there was a really big break in the long convoy of trucks. I was able to safely pull over into the slow lane and start getting back to the speed limit.

I expected the cruiser to whistle by me, but it didn't. When I looked in the mirror it was still behind me – in the slow lane – and with the lights still flashing it was slowing as I slowed. So I stopped and he pulled up right behind me.

I raised my hands in the air and wondered 'What's going on?'

In my side mirror I saw the OPP officer get out of the cruiser, adjust his hat, and walk towards my vehicle.

I was nervous. I didn't even wait for him to speak. I said something like, 'I was trying to get out of your way, I thought you were after somebody else.'

And that's what I really did think. I had never been pulled over. I had been driving for only three months.

He gets to the driver's side door and asks, "You know why I pulled you over?"

"I don't know why you were after me."

He tells me that when I pulled out of the restaurant I was not wearing a seatbelt.

# Shawn Brush

"I never wear a seatbelt. I don't wear a seatbelt because of my chest. It restricts me."

He goes back to the cruiser with my license and I am sitting there white-knuckling the steering wheel because I am thinking the worst. What's going to happen to me now?

I've heard about drivers trying to outrun the cops. In a high-speed chase. The courts are not easy on them – and they usually get a lot of media attention. I don't need this.

It occurred to me that they might just take me off the road right there and then and cart me off to jail in the cruiser. I guess I have seen too many cops and robbers movies.

He strolls back to me. I try to look calm and nonchalant.

"You know  you are pretty good-looking guy with a shave and a haircut" he says while looking at my driver's licence. I said "Thanks."

He said I was free to go. He told me to drive safely. And that was that.

He understood why I don't wear a seatbelt and I have thought about this officer often since then, realising how sensible and reasonable he had been. He could have argued the seatbelt issue and said he was just doing his job and ticketed me so I would have to go to court to argue my side. But he didn't.

And he could have thrown the book at me if he suspected I had been trying to outrun him. After all, the needle on my car hit 160 km/h before it was buried. But he didn't give me a ticket. Not even for speeding.

It was an interesting experience. It was the first time I had been pulled over by the police.

So there I was on the 401 and I had to get down to Windsor and go through the tunnel and come out in Detroit.

At the border, U.S. immigration officer say, "Where are you going?"

"Sudbury." It was the first place that came into my mind. Don't ask me why, but I didn't think they would let me go if I said I was going to Wyoming.

He says, "Okay,  have a good time."

Just like that. It was easy.

I get driving through the interstate through the city and get to the other side of Detroit. It starts raining – and I mean really raining. It was pouring down. Just

# The Krooked Cowboy

My friend, Bert Steen, wrote this song about my trip to Wyoming.

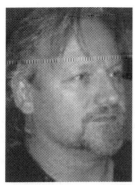

Bert Steen

## Wyoming

Well I think I'm gonna drive on back to Wyoming again
Can somebody tell me
why I always have to be
stuck out on the losing end?
I fell in love or so it seems
with the girl of my dreams
she never wanted to be more than a friend
So I think I'm gonna have
to drive on back
to the state of Wyoming again

Last time I went
I come home without a cent
and a memory that wasn't too clear
I told a friend that I was going
to somewhere in Wyoming
said "I'll bring you back a souvenir"

So I think I'm gonna drive on back to Wyoming again
can somebody tell me
why I always have to be
stuck out on the losing end?
I fell in love or so it seems
with the girl of my dreams
she never wanted to be more than a friend
so I think I'm gonna have
to drive on back
to the state of Wyoming again
I got my Martin guitar
in my Cadillac car
and I'm goin' to Wyoming again.

**Bert Steen**

like a cloudburst. I looked at my gas gauge and it was on 'empty.' I realized then that I didn't have any money.

I pull off the highway in some small town and I start thinking what I am going to do. I can't go back I am out of gas.

I can't even make a phone call, I didn't have a cellphone. Then I thought about the credit card. I see a bank with a drive-through bank machine.

I put the credit card into the machine. I was nervous. I wondered if it will work. It is Canadian, and I am in the United States. Sure enough it works. Whew! I get a cash advance of $100 American.

First thing I did was buy some junk food and fill up the gas tank. Now I'm headed west.

The rain hasn't let up. The more I drive the worse it gets. There are many cars in the ditch. I think I can make good time because nobody is on the highway and I drive down through Michigan to Gary, Indiana and the rain lets up for a while.

I am cruising along the Interstate and get around Illinois, just outside Chicago.

I got off the highway and I got lost and I ended up in Joliette. So I eventually find my way back to the highway, and decided to stay on the highway the rest of the way. No more detours.

I cross over the Mississippi and it is still raining and blowing. The wind is really blowing and there is nobody on Interstate 80. I thought this was strange. It goes from the east coast through to San Francisco and I expected it would be packed, but there is nobody on it. The sky is pitch black, it is dark and the wind is blowing and I have to hang on with both hands because the wind is hitting the side of the car.

The radio quits on me and I am getting tired now because I have been driving all day and all night. It is Tuesday morning. So I decide to pull over.

I am in Iowa and I pull into a truck stop - one of those big stops in the Midwest with down-home folks, homemade pie, great atmosphere. There are a couple of waitresses working the nightshift, a couple of truckers and couple of locals.

I order a bowl of soup. They are all listening to the radio. There is a tornado warning in effect for Iowa, Nebraska, and Kansas. It seemed to be concentrated just where I was at the truck stop.

# The Krooked Cowboy

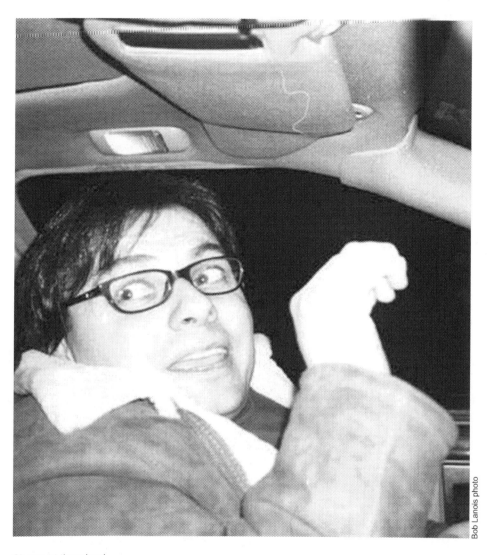

Shawn at the wheel.

# Shawn Brush

They ask me, "How did you get here?"

They wanted to know what the weather was like where I had been travelling.

I told them there was no one on the highway.

I had been totally oblivious to what was going on until I heard that radio. I started shaking and I went outside and lay down in the backseat to grab some shut eye.

When I wake up, the sun's up. I get some more supplies to eat and drink as I drive.

The radio is back on air, but there's a lot of static.

I get to DesMoines, Iowa, and go off to Sioux City.

There is a bluff that overlooks the two cities, Sioux City, Iowa and Omaha, Nebraska.

Coming into Omaha, I hear Bob Seger and the Silver Bullet Band on the radio and they are doing *Turn The Page* and the first line of the lyric is *"On a long and lonesome highway east of Omaha..."*, so it was a memorable moment driving into Omaha listening to Bob Seger singing about that same part of the world.

I decided to stretch my legs in Omaha. I go downtown and end up walking around a shopping mall. I must have looked like the Mountain Man of Wyoming, with several days of beard. I walked into a restaurant and everyone was looking at me.

Soon I was back in the car and driving again.

The car starts making a funny noise. Just what I need, car trouble. Thousands of miles away from home.

It was a familiar noise to me. I had first heard it back at the truck stop in Iowa. When I shut off the car I could hear a whirrrrrrring sound and I wondered what it was. I had never heard it before. I put it down to driving all day and I thought maybe it was cooling off.

So I didn't pay much attention to it in Iowa.

After I had eaten and slept I could hear the sound in the background.

However, the car seemed be running well, so I didn't worry about it and kept heading west. But it was not getting any quieter and then a different noise appeared. It sounded like metal grinding.

# The Krooked Cowboy

First thing to come into my mind when I heard that metal sound was that I needed oil - fast.

So I pull into a 76 truck stop, run in, grab the first oil thing I see, throw my credit card on the table, run back out to the car, lift the hood, get the oil cap off, it is still super hot and pour the oil in.

One quart. Two quarts. Three. It was dangerously low. After a minute I shut it off and let it cool down.

I hear this whirring sound again.

I didn't worry about it.

Then I noticed that my antenna was broken. It was dangling on the side of the car. When did that happen? It was one of those extendable ones.

I still hear the whirring sound.

Whatever it was I didn't have time to investigate. I have got to keep moving. I have got to get to Wyoming.

I am in Nebraska and it is flat and straight and the highway follows the Platte River. It is a different landscape than Iowa that has small rolling hills and lots of farmland. Iowa stinks like manure from one end to the other, especially through the farm areas. It is the smell of money, I guess, and I am sure people get used to it. But for me it was almost nauseating. It wasn't just the odd whiff here and there that forced you to keep the windows closed, it was everywhere. It was constant. And it didn't matter that the windows were shut tight.

Nebraska almost lulls you to sleep. It's flat. Hardly any change of scenery for mile after mile, hour after hour.

When you look down at the speedometer and see you are going 120 or 160 kilometres an hour.

You slow down to the 65 mph speed limit, but after about 10 minutes you are doing 140 km/h. It is just monotonous and you just want to get to the end of it.

I just want to get some place to see something. My plan was to stop in Ogallala, the cowboy capital of Nebraska back in the 1870s and 1880s.

All along the highway there were signs to the museums about the Pony Express, Buffalo Bill Cody, Wild Bill Hickok. There were all kinds of tourist traps – and I am sure plenty of souvenirs.

# Shawn Brush

Most of the wild west towns have a Boot Hill. It was a name given to cemeteries where gunfighters were buried, or where those frontier men had died violently, or 'died with their boots on' as the expression goes. Ogallala had its own boot hill. Ogallala is an Indian word from the Oglala band of the Dakota Sioux and it means 'scatter one's own' and it has legends. I'd heard about it in the movies. I had read about it in books. Here I am in Ogallala. Wow.'

I needed some money so I went downtown and found a bank machine and I picked up a disposable camera from a truck stop where I had stopped to eat dinner. They had no running water in the restaurant. I was in the wild west. I went into the washroom, to wash my hands and no running water.

I asked for a drink of water.

No we don't have any running water.

I was downtown Ogallala. There was an Indian fellow. There was a bar on the street. There was nobody downtown. It was a western town with wide sidewalks. There was a tavern.

The Indian was lying on the street in the gutter, hammered, passed out cold. I took a picture of him. I thought wow. That's the real west.

I went and booked a room at the Best Western beside the highway and went into my room and laid down, but I couldn't get to sleep because I was thinking I had to get that souvenir.

They must have something around here. I got up and looked out the front door of the motel and it is one of those motels where you step out of your room right to your parked car.

The door opened in the room next to me and a guy in his mid-50s came out.

"How are you doing?" I said.

"Not bad."

"Where are you from?

"I am a local here." He was a lawyer.

"Where are you from?"

"Toronto."

"What are you doing?"

"My friend didn't believe I'd come, so I did."

76

# The Krooked Cowboy

The lawyer gave me a card, adding, "If you need any help."

Unfortunately, I lost the card. I wish I still had it. I forget the guy's name.

There was a truck stop across the field from the front of the Best Western. I thought they must have souvenirs there. They only had tee-shirts. And only for Nebraska.

He said you need something for Wyoming, you'll have to go to Wyoming.

I went back to the room and put everything in the car and headed for Wyoming.

I am 127 miles from the Wyoming border.

I figured I can be in Wyoming by midnight. I am tired. I have been in the car two days. The last thing on my brain was 127 miles. I am driving along and I get to Pines Bluff, Wyoming about midnight. It's just a little place. Just a dot on the map.

They have the same size dots as the towns and cities, but Pines Bluff is smaller than the dots on the map would have you think.

So I pull off the highway and there is a little gas station.

I gas up and grab a banner and a couple of little knickknacks and trinkets that say Wyoming and a map.

I pay for stuff, get outside and there is a signpost with distances to a number of different places – Seattle, Salt Lake City, Texas, Kansas, Las Vegas, San Francisco, Chicago, Detroit and Toronto.

Chicago and San Francisco were about the same distance. For a moment it enters my mind to keep heading west.

Then, for the first time in a few days, I called on good sense to make a decision for me. No more of this gallivanting around. I had better get back home. Nobody knows where I am. I had just picked up and left and my mom needs the car to get to work.

So I jump in the car and start driving – east!

I remember pulling out of that gas station and getting on the on-ramp of the highway and looking over my left-shoulder at that little stop in the distance in the lights where I had finally got my souvenirs of Wyoming.

It is now about 12:30 in the morning. I have got to get back to my motel to get some sleep for the big ride east.

# Shawn Brush

The next thing I remember is red lights. Bright red lights. Brake lights. They are just solid. They are just a few feet in front of me and I hit the brakes and luckily there is nobody else beside me or around me, or following me. As I come to, I realise these are red tail lights and they are now pulling away from me. They are on the bottom of a transport trailer.

The car came to a complete stop after I had hit the brakes and skidded, turning a little bit sideways, pointing to the side of the road. I had scared myself, so after stopping a few seconds to catch my breath and get my bearings I realised I was close to an off-ramp. I thought I would get off the highway for a little while.

It turned out it was my exit to the motel. I had locked the keys in my hotel room so I had to wake up the desk clerk.

I went to my room and just lay there and it didn't dawn on me at the time, but I drove 100-odd miles and I didn't have any memory of driving and then stopping at the exact exit I needed to be.

I think that single moment in my life is one of the weirdest. Very strange. There were other spiritual things I was going through on that trip that are hard to explain. Not visions and hallucinations, but feeling a certain connection with another part of the universe. With an exchange of powers and talents in a spiritual sense.

I have thought often about what made me stop on the highway and I put it down to a guardian angel, fate, what is meant to be, or self-hypnosis, whatever you want to call it. Somebody was looking out for me in the spirit world because I was in Wyoming and from the Wyoming border it was 127 miles to my hotel.

One of the things that was in the back of my mind when I said Wyoming was they have medicine wheels that are stones cast into the ground, famous medicine wheels in Wyoming. That's why I said Wyoming. But I didn't go that far.

When I got to the hotel and shut off the car it was still making that whirrrring sound every stop. It wouldn't stop.

I got into the hotel room and fell asleep. I was just drained. I felt that I just had to get back.

It's not fair to do this to my family and friends. No matter what I am going through it is not right. I didn't think to phone and say anything. I just thought I had to get back.

# The Krooked Cowboy

I had a good sleep and got up early.

The car started, but that engine noise was still there. I thought I had better get it looked at. There was a little place down the road with one guy working in this single bay garage.

I asked him to check it out.

He listened to it.

He said that sounds like your cooling fan motor. You don't want to be driving through the prairies without your cooling motor. Where are you going?

You are going to overheat

Now he's got me panicked.

"Can you fix it."

"I can but I have to order the parts and they won't get here for a couple of days."

He tells me of a dealership in North Platte, Nebraska, about 140 miles up the road.

The interstate practically follows the trail west used by the wagon trains.

The North Platte dealership is right in the middle of a cornfield. It was just like out of a movie. The car is still making the whirrring noise.

The mechanic can't find anything wrong. He has never heard the noise before. Then he sees the broken antenna. It's an automatic antenna, so when it broke in two it would not go up and down, but it was continuing to go around.

He just disconnected the wire.

That's when it dawned on me that the wind must have broken the antenna.in the first place, back during the tornado warning. No one was on the highway and I was having to hang onto the steering wheel with two hands because the wind was shaking my car.

If there was a tornado with me that night, I didn't see it. But there must have been something awfully close, something powerful enough for the wind to rip the antenna off the side of the car.

I had the antenna motor unhooked and started driving down the highway.

I was beginning to feel exhausted. The stressful situations were getting to me.

I get to the eastern part of Iowa and the skies cloud over and they still have

# Shawn Brush

storm warnings.

As I cross over the Misssissippi it starts raining.

I have been driving all day (Wednesday) and I am in Illinois, belting along at 65 mph and I am boxed in when the cruiser lights come up.

I am speeding to get out of the way of the guy who has been tailgaiting me. I just wanted him to get past. So sure enough he has pulled me over because I am speeding now.

It was one of those cold, nasty, damp, dismal wet rains. It was late. It was after midnight. It was Wednesday night and Thursday morning. I wait for the police officer to appear at the driver's door. I look back and all the lights are on. It has now been about 10 minutes since I stopped – and still no policeman.

I don't want to get out because it was so miserable.

I roll down the window and start the car, stick my head out of the window with both hands up.

He gets out of the cruiser with gun drawn. "Where are you going? Who are you? Give me your licence and registrations."

That was intimidating for me. However, I kept my cool and shouted I was just trying to get home to Toronto.

He takes my license, checks it out and comes back and tells me to "have a good night." He lets me go on my way.

I drove through Indiana and into Michigan and then stopped at some truck stop, pulled around into a quiet spot, climbed into the back seat and got some shut eye. When I awoke a few hours later it had stopped raining, so I got back on the road again.

I got to just outside of Detroit and stopped and had something to eat, drove over the border into Canada without any problem, and rolled along the 401 to London.

I had to stop. I was just whipped.

I didn't rest for long, but enough to refresh me and start out for Ancaster. When I got there to deliver the souvenirs, no one was home.

However, the front door was open so I took out all the souvenirs and I went in and laid them all over. I took out my map and placed it on the table with the Wyoming banner on top of it. I also had a newspaper from Denver, Colorado

# The Krooked Cowboy

I picked up.

Then I drove to my home, fell asleep for a few hours and got up and felt pretty good and went to the Bluegrass jam. I even played some songs,

I had driven just over 7,000 kilometres in five or six days.

# Shawn Brush

Shawn and his sister, Michelle, spent a lot of their childhood riding horses.

# 10

# Selling SIN in the mall

I was pretty much broke because I was just putting gas in the car and eating and living and going from place to place experiencing things. It was time to sit down. Those bills from the credit card started to come in. I owed a pretty good chunk of change that I had racked up in a short period of time. I figured I had a few options. One was to go back to school.

I didn't like the idea of commuting so I ended up finding out about some correspondence courses. I decided that because I had all this free time on my hands, instead of just doing one course I would do two courses.

So I was looking into jobs I could handle and one thing that interested me was computer mathematics. It was something that I knew nothing about. I signed up and started getting some packages in the mail.

Then I had been doing some reading and studying about industries taking off in Ontario and in Canada and I found out about fish farming. There was a course in zoology and biology about fish farming. I started thinking all you needed was a swimming pool, holding tanks and a truck comes along and picks up all the fish. If it is that simple, I thought, I can do that. If it were that simple I figure a lot more people would be doing it and making easy money.

Fish farming sounded like something for me. I was really interested in it and it had proven to be an industry that is already working well in different parts of the world and here in Canada.

It is being looked at for its economics, its resources and wildlife and the health of the environment, the animals and beyond our own consumption into the big environment.

So for a few months I was heavily involved in learning all about it and I got kind of isolated. I was by myself and just studying and didn't have any money so I couldn't go out and do anything.

It was a quiet time. Kind of frustrating at the same time, but I was pursuing this academic level. I needed a break one day and I ended up going out to the mall where my dad had a booth set up. I can't remember what he was selling, it may have been the Kraft-matic beds.

There would be different things set up in the mall every week.

It is kind of like a trade show that goes through the malls. There will be a cultural and craft show one week and then kitchen accessories with slicers and dicers.

It is a pretty common sight. This particular day there was a booth set up and there was a woman with a small machine that sat on the table for stamping, embossing and doing a metal card for ID.

The thing they were selling was a Social Insurance card. If you already had your plastic government issued SIN card they would take your number and put it on the metal card and you needed to sign it and it was fairly inexpensive, like $7 or $8.

I saw this. It appealed to me because I could sell these things sitting down. I talked to the lady who owned the machine and ran the booth and then the guy who supplied the cards showed up. I talked to them both and asked how much a machine was and if it was something I could start.

It looked like a pretty good business made just for me.

My mom and dad offered to loan me the money to get set up in business.

So this was a whole new avenue for me and it was something that I could immediately start making money, and pay off my debts and be self-sustaining and get out in the world and do things.

# The Krooked Cowboy

With money from my mom and dad I bought the machine, a batch of cards, a table, a chair and an easel.

I had a sign made 'Get your SIN card - a permanent record of your SIN number.'

I had some Canadian flags on it to kind of make it look Canadian and official.

I had to get a fire retardant piece of cloth around the table not just so it looked good, but for insurance purposes.

I had to take out a $1 million liability insurance policy as a minimum to work at any trade shows in the malls.

It was January 1993 and I started that little business. The first couple of places I went into were close to home, like Burlington, Oakville, Milton and I worked pretty darn hard.

I went from being in the home doing nothing, being a night owl, that's my nature sometimes, to getting up at 7:30 in the morning and getting a ride with all my gear and setting up in the mall for 9 o'clock.

If my mom had to go work, she would take the car. Either she or dad would pick me up at 9 p.m.

It was a full day. It was a real experience to go from lounging on the couch and doing things at my leisure. I was working hard at the studying. And I was trying to do the studying now when I had free time, but there wasn't much free time.

I had to learn to sell.

I would get there and maybe have enough change in my pocket for lunch. So I would have to make up my dinner money by working. But I would have to pay the rent for that space.

I got it down to a science that I would work the first two days and try to pay off my rent for the week and then after that everything was gravy and money in my pocket. It would pay for my lunch, dinner and other expenses, like gas.

It was quite a transition to make.

Then I remember one Wednesday night, I wanted to go to play some music because I hadn't played music in the bluegrass jam for a few weeks. I missed it.

I wanted to go out. I had worked a lot of 9 to 9 days.

# Shawn Brush

I had a short day on the Wednesday, packing up early. I borrowed the car and went to the bluegrass jam session.

All my life when I was going to school I always had a ride. Always had someone that I could depend on.

I didn't need to depend on myself to get there and get me home.

When I started doing that little business of my own, my job was an eye-opener for me because I went down to play on the Wednesday night and I was tired. I never considered myself disabled or handicapped but it was a time in my life that the guys I saw playing all the time all worked day jobs and they got out once a week to play music. They packed up early and they were done at 10 p.m. because they had to get up at 5 a.m. and do a shift.

Just for them to come out it was a good deal of enjoyment. So I experienced that from their point of view, but working all day was much more taxing on me physically because I was literally pushing myself to the extreme.

That night I played music, I really enjoyed it. I went home, dropped off to sleep and when I got up the next day I was tired. I was really tired. I was over-tired.

My mom drove me in and dropped me off. I was there for the day.

I had some breakfast before going off to work in Oakville at Trafalgar Square. I set up beside the engraving booth where they cut keys and I had my machine set up but I was just dragging my feet.

It was one of those times when you have got to bite the bullet. So I got in there and started working and come about 11 a.m. I was in pretty rough shape and I was really hungry.

I went over to the restaurant and had a BLT or grilled cheese, I was still hungry. I ate two of them. I may have eaten three.

I was exhausted. I came out of the restaurant and I felt that I was just going to pass out. I felt that I had to lie down.

There wasn't really anywhere for me to go. People were around my booth and they were waiting to get a card.

I wasn't in any shape to be with them. I went over to the barber shop to get a haircut and sit in the chair and just relax.

I could feel my heart pounding. I was sitting there. I knew something was wrong because my heart was going faster and faster. It was racing.

# The Krooked Cowboy

I looked at the girl and said I had to lie down on the floor. I said you had better call an ambulance. It sort of freaked her out.

I said my heart is racing. I can't relax

She ran out of the barber shop and ran over to get some help. Someone said there is some guy in there and he is having a heart attack, He came to look and he said, "I know this guy. He's a friend of mine".

By that time my heart rate had gone down and I felt just tired. There wasn't anything anyone could do. I was coherent. I was breathing normally. But my heart was just racing and racing.

The ambulance showed up and the paramedics came in and took my blood pressure. My heart was doing over 160 beats and I was lying down flat on my back, breathing slowly. I was like a humming bird. It just shot up to that high range and it wouldn't go back down. I figured it was because I was pushing myself.

Then all of a sudden my heart beat went down, down, down and my blood pressure was just through the roof.

I just relaxed.

A friend of mine, Scott Apted who I went to college with, lived right around the corner from Trafalgar Square and it was he who had come to see me just at the time I was lying on the floor of the barber shop.

By the time my heart rate had gone down I felt tired. They wanted to take me to the hospital and I didn't want to go. I thought I am going to be okay. I didn't think I needed to go to the hospital. I was scared to go to the hospital, you never know what they are going to do.

So I asked Scott to take me to his house. I went in his car and rested on his couch. I fell asleep for about four hours.

I woke up and he made me a huge sandwich and I ate that and ate another sandwich, I was still hungry.

He said, "Are you okay?"

I was pale as a ghost.

The rest is what I needed.

I said I had better get back over to the mall to go to work.

I finished at 9 o'clock that night.

# Shawn Brush

It was one of those days. It was a really bad day. My mom came to pick me up and she came in to get me because I wasn't outside waiting.

I went home that night, did my books, went to bed, got up the next day and went to work and realized that if I am going to do this there is not going to be any music.

I just couldn't even do one night.

I would have to be committed to doing just the job. I was working hard and it was starting to pay off so I stuck it out. That was February and then March and then I got it down to where it was only worthwhile to do three or four days – Wednesday to Saturday and sometimes a Sunday.

There were weeks that I went by myself into little places like the Milton mall. The first time I went there I was sitting in front of the book store by the food court and it was going really slowly. The mall was really dead.

As I was sitting there most of the day I went to buy something to read at  the book store. I took some of my zoology books and studied there when I could, when it was quiet. One day I was sitting in the mall and kind of thinking I am not making any money, I hadn't even made my rent and I had been staying there from 9 in the morning until 9 at night. I tell you that is a lonesome job for anybody.

I was sitting reading my book and there was a guy standing in front of me and he was reading the sign. And I looked at him and said, "Can I help you?"

He didn't look at me.

I said 'Hello' again and he appeared to be ignoring me.

Then he looks at my table and he looks at me and I started talking to him and started making my sales pitch. He looks away and he looks down at the table and he picks up one of the ID cards.

He looks at it and he looks at me and I started making my sales pitch again and he throws the card on the table and walks away. I thought that was really weird and the behaviour of people is a real study working in a mall.

A couple of hours go by and there is another guy standing in front of my table. I start talking to him and he's not looking at me either, but he's looking at the cards. He looks at the sign and I am talking away to him. He looks at me and sort of nods his head, then walks away.

Really weird. I have only had two customers. It is 4 o'clock in the afternoon

# The Krooked Cowboy

and both of them had not said a word to me. They acted very strange.

Then another guy came along and he's standing there looking at different things. He looks at the cards, looks at me, reads the sign and looks at the cards again and walks away.

I am talking to him, but he doesn't answer me. He walks away.

I am sitting there scratching my head. That went on the whole day and part of the next day.

It is the middle of the week now and I haven't made a single sale. I am losing money. I am going to have to work really hard somewhere else to make up that loss.

I look up and I recognize one of the guys who was at my table and he sits down at the food court. He is with a couple of people and they all start doing sign language. They are all deaf. The school for the deaf is next door to the mall in Milton.

I kind of chuckle to myself.

I was right next to the bookstore, so I knew what I had to do. I needed a book on sign language. They had one. It was about seven or eight dollars. It showed how to say 'hello,' 'goodbye' and 'thank you' and the most important thing, 'only $7.99.'

I sat down at the table. I studied it. I practiced the signs. I was ready. I just sat there and waited for the next person to come along.

One of the guys who had been there earlier was back. He was wearing a lumber jacket and looked like a tough guy. He was deaf, totally deaf. He looked at the cards and he looked at me and he looked at the sign and I didn't say anything and didn't do anything. He looked at me one last time. As I did the sign for '$7.99' he looked at me and he had the biggest grin on his face. All I did was that one little thing, I said '$7.99' in sign language.

He pulled out his wallet, put down a $10 bill and pulled out his SIN and I made him a card and he signed it and put it in his wallet. I gave him his change and he went away with that big grin still on his face.

I felt that was good and I thought if any more customers come in from the school for the deaf I know exactly how to deal with them. How to make them feel comfortable.

The next morning at about 10 o'clock the same guy came up and he had his whole family with him and they all got cards. He had gone home and told them about it. They were all deaf.

Then another guy came up and he got a card. All I did was sign 'hello' along with '$7.99' and 'thank you.' That's all I had to do. The easiest sales I ever made.

They just came in droves. I really cleaned up.

There was a little mall on Queenston Road in Stoney Creek, just up the street from the bowling alley where I used to hang out. It had a Fortinos in it and a Zellers. It was a little funny-shaped mall; there was a bar and a coffee shop and donut shop. I phoned the mall and said I would like to set up a table to sell my product.

The mall manager asked me what I did and I told him about SIN cards.

The whole thing with selling these cards were that you are not an official employee of the government. It is not an official card. You are not issuing a SIN number. It is just like writing your number down on a piece of paper, but the card was made to look very official. It is on a brass plate and it has the Canadian flag on it and it says 'Social Insurance Number.' You sign it with a pen made out of soft metal to enable you to engrave your name on it. You put the card into a machine and it stamps your name and number onto it.

I got to be really good at it. During the whole sales pitch though you couldn't tell them that you worked for the government.

The government issues these plastic cards and they break. Construction workers have trouble with the plastic cards and truck drivers sit on them in their trucks and break them all the time.

Whenever they see this permanent record they didn't ask whether it was official they just bought it and stuck it in their wallet and forgot about it.

It was kind of a scam in a way, but in another way it was an honest thing. I didn't lie about it. Some made their own assumptions about it and bought it.

A lot of guys would buy it because the metal card not only replaced their broken SIN card, but it saved them money by not having to replace their plastic card every year or two. It kept their wallets straight and kept all their other cards from getting folded and bent and broken.

It was a good product and it was fairly inexpensive and they didn't have to wait in a line and then get it mailed to them.

# The Krooked Cowboy

At that one little mall on Queenston Road I did very well. Extremely well. Better than I did anywhere else. They didn't have anyone else in the mall, just me.

I was set up between the coffee shop and Fortinos.

I was having an extremely good week – really doing well.

I guess there was a bitter rivalry between the manager of the mall and one of the businesses. I didn't know it, but the actual government Social Insurance office was in that mall. It was way in the back and that's why they put me right in the front.

I had no knowledge that the government office was in the back.

Guys were coming in with their construction boots on and they were in a hurry to get to the government office. They would come in and see me first and would be looking for a new SIN card because theirs had broken.

I was cleaning up. I answered all of the questions and I didn't have to do much talking. I was asked very difficult questions. Never anywhere else was I asked these kind of questions.

There was a guy in a blue suit. He was probably in his mid to late 40s and he was watching me and listening to me. He would go in the coffee shop and he would disappear then he would come back again. The next day he was around.

He would walk away, but he was always in close enough range that he could hear what I was saying.

After about two or three days he walked up to me and he said, "You know you are the best person I have ever seen do this."

"What do you mean?"

"I work for the government for fraud for Social Insurance and we bust guys like you all the time for making false statements, selling the card as an actual government card."

He said, "You have your language right down pat. You are the best I have ever seen at this." He told me they had the official office right there in the mall.

He got pulled out of his office because they had no business all week. The guys were coming in, but they were coming straight to me. It was kind of funny that I was taking the government business away and I did it totally legitimately.

## Shawn Brush

That was fun.

Some other funny things happened.

I remember a lady came up and got a card from me one day. She had a really unusual last name.

I said I needed a piece of ID so I can copy it correctly. She gave me her driver's licence.

I copied it down, checked it and re-checked it before I made the card. She signed it and paid me.

The next day she came back and she said I had made a mistake on her card.

"I did?"

"Yes, there is a letter that is wrong."

"Oh, are you sure?"

I looked at it, and I remembered doing it from her driver's licence.

She gave me a different piece of ID.

She was very insistent that I made a mistake.

She gave me her birth certificate and she said, "Look, it (the ID card) is wrong."

I said the ID was not wrong, but her driver's license was wrong. Her name had been incorrect on her driver's license for years, but she had never noticed.

It was interesting running into these different people and personalities.

They would assume that you were working for the government because they would see a guy sitting in a suit at a table very officious-looking with the flags and the sign and people would just assume that you work for the government . . . or it was a charity because I was small.

I remember one guy coming up to me and saying it was good to see 'you people' working.

I got a lot of really good experiences in that short time I did that little business. I learned a lot. It built up my confidence level.

I learned how to sell myself.

Shawn with two of his friends and fellow musicians, Terry Sumsion and the late Roadkill Bill.

# Shawn Brush

Shawn at the Staircase Theatre with Steve Ashley, a friend, musician and producer.

# 11

# Good times in Nashville

When you are a country music fan Nashville is a place you want to go. When you are a musician it is Mecca.

The first time I went to Nashville I was 18 and it was one of those weekend bus trips. You leave Thursday night and you are back in time for work Monday morning.

I was just turning 18. It was a week or so before my birthday and I went down on the bus with a group of people I had not met before.

I took my guitar. You never know where you'll get a chance to play, or who will be watching.

Well, it was a good thing that I didn't know anyone on the bus. By the time we got to Detroit I was drunk. I don't remember much about the trip down. I slept pretty well all the way on that 12 to 14-hour bus trip.

One of the first places I saw was the Ryman Auditorium in downtown Nashville. This was just a few years before Nashville is what it is today with the old downtown area cleaned up and the Ryman renovated.

Downtown Nashville was one of the places where they had told us not to be alone after dark.

# Shawn Brush

The bus tour was staying out at a hotel in Hendersonville. There was a bar at the end of the hotel on the second floor. Even though the drinking age was 21 and I was 17 going on 18, I managed to get into the bar. I watched what everyone else was doing. You just say you will have a beer, it doesn't matter what brand it is really.

I went to another bar, Tootsie's Orchid Lounge, regarded as the world famous backdoor into the Grand Ol' Opry. Hank Williams, Willie Nelson, everybody who is somebody in the country music field has played there. They always have somebody sitting and playing music in there. From what I remember they don't serve liquor, just beer. And they only had two kinds, Budweiser and Coors, if I remember correctly.

So here I am, 17 in Nashville, back at the hotel where we were staying, and there is a band playing on the stage. So I go up to the bar.

Bartender says, "What will you have?"

"A beer."

Then I had another.

"Where are you from?"

"Canada"

"How old are you?"

"19."

That was the wrong answer. I had not done my due diligence. While 19 was the legal drinking age where I was from in Ontario, in Nashville you had to be 21. I got picked up by the scruff of the neck and booted out the back door.

So there I am in the back alley of this bar. It is open until three or four o'clock in the morning. The band is pretty good so I am sitting there listening. Along comes a couple of girls with fishnet stockings and bustiers, looking like they were there to do business – and they were.

They asked me what I was doing and I explained I had just got kicked out of the bar. They were southern girls and they were very friendly. "Just hang out here sweetheart and we'll go in and get you a drink."

They kept bringing me out a drink and once in a while and they would come out and sit with me. So I had a lot of fun.

The next day I wasn't feeling too well. My head was hurting. No prizes for

# The Krooked Cowboy

guessing why. I stayed around the hotel for the first part of the day. When I got feeling better I went out and did some more sightseeing.

That night rolled around and they had a different bartender at the bar I had got kicked out of the day before. So the guy says to me, "How old are you?"

This time I was smarter than the night before - "21."

So I said I was 21. Funny, isn't it that we would lie, put our reputation on the line, all for the sake of a beer.

He gave me a beer and didn't ask for any ID, so I stayed there all night with some of the people from the bus and got pretty loaded.

One guy said he was having a party back in his room and I should bring the guitar over. Some of the girls from the bus trip were headed over.

This guy's name was Lucky Chuckie. He was a truck driver from some place in Tennessee. He had homemade plum wine in 7-Up bottles and we were drinking this wine. It might as well have been moonshine.

He was phoning people long distance all night long on his credit card and and we were laughing. Everyone else had passed out and there was just me and Lucky Chuckie and he was still phoning his friends all over the continent. And I was playing the guitar.

At that point I realised I needed to get some sleep or eat something. Chuckie said there was a pancake house right across the road and wanted to go there.

It was 5 or 6 in the morning.

Right where the hotel was, they were building an overpass for the highway, and there was a field and a pancake house was on the other side. Chuckie wanted to drive, but I said, "No way. I am not going to drive with you."

"I will walk straight across the field and I will meet you at the pancake house."

It was still dark and had been raining all weekend. It was muddy. Really yucky. I couldn't see very well, but I started off across the field. In the middle of the field, where it was darkest, I fell into a six-foot-deep hole.

Luckily, I could see headlights shining over the field. It was this guy Lucky Chuckie now driving onto the field. He had seen me one minute and the next he didn't see me. He couldn't hear me yelling for help because he was in the car. He got out of the car and I could see his shadow walking towards me.

97

# Shawn Brush

He was yelling, "Where did you go? Where did you go?"

"I am in a hole, straight ahead of you. Watch that you don't fall in."

He almost fell in, he was laughing so much.

He had to lie down on the ground in the mud and reach down and grab my hand and pull me out of the hole. I had mud from my ankle to my forehead. I was a mess.

He said, "Let's go and get those pancakes."

I said, "You know what. I ain't hungry any more. I am going back to my room, take a hot bath and get some sleep.

He said, "Okay."

I went back to the hotel, soaked in a hot bath, got the shakes I was so chilled. When I got into bed and began to warm up, the sun was coming up.

It seemed as though I had just closed my eyes when the phone rang. It was checkout time. The bus is leaving soon.

I get up and pack my stuff. I am not feeling very good. This is the third day without any rest.

I get on the bus and they had planned a riverboat cruise for the day on this paddle wheeler, the General Jackson, which sails the Cumberland River from downtown Nashville. I tell you, that was the longest boat ride I ever had in my life. Someone took a picture and I was as white as a ghost. Then we got back on the bus, I pass out and I wake up back in Canada.

I had slept upside down on the bus seat and my back was as stiff as a board. Went home, had a sleep, got up the next day and went to work.

Well, the bus trip is the way many get to see Nashville. I also got to see Nashville in a very special way. My buddy Larry Sinai won a trip to Nashville for the day on Oct. 11, 1989 on country Radio 640 CFGM. They had a radio booth in Nashville and they were flying contest winners down every day – just for the day.

Larry called me on the Tuesday and told me to listen to the radio in the morning because he thought he was going to win. I got up at 5:30 and turned on the radio and sure enough he won.

They said who are you taking to Nashville and he said, "I am going to take my friend, Shawn, it is his birthday today." They picked us up at Larry's place

Larry Sinai sings Happy Birthday to me on the air in Nashville. The CFGM announcer is on the right.

around noon and we got up to the airport and they flew us to Nashville on American Airlines.

Larry wanted to bring his fiddle and his guitar.

It is about a 90-minute flight from Toronto to Nashville and we got into the drink on the plane and had quite a few cocktails.

We stumbled off the plane laughing and giggling and a little intoxicated. Oh no, it's going to be one of those days.

A guy was waiting for us with a sign with our names on it.

We get to the hotel where the radio station had its booth set up in one of the rooms. Radio stations from all across the continent were set up in the hotel but I think CFGM was the only one from Canada.

They were doing a live remote simulcast every day from Nashville.

What happens is the big country stars and the up-and-comers who have big songs on the radio come in and get to talk to all the radio stations and do a couple of jingles for them.

## Shawn Brush

That day the Judds were scheduled to come in but they didn't make it. Some of the other people I met that day included Marty Stuart, Eddy Arnold and Tammy Wynette.

The radio station wanted us on the air, but we were too intoxicated. They had a large spread buffet and kept pouring coffee into us. But no more booze.

Meeting Tammy Wynette in Nashville was a big thrill for Shawn.

We kept on insisting on more drinks but all they would give us was black coffee.

Towards the end of the afternoon they wrapped up all the radio stuff and took us for dinner and we had some drinks and then they put us back on the plane to Toronto.

More drinks on the plane and we ended up back at Larry's house in Mississauga around midnight.

We were so wound up we went to Larry Matson's bar on the South Service Road in Burlington. Larry was a Canadian country singer and he had a couple of records about 20 years ago. His daughter Laura Matson sang

I saw Little Jimmy Dickens, Bill Monroe and Jason McCoy at Larry's bar over the years.

But the night we had come home from Nashville we closed down the place then went back to Larry's house and it was about three in the morning when I fell asleep.

It was about 6 a.m. when there was a knock on the front door. It was the guys from the radio station. I didn't know what was going on and he said 'you guys were the big contest winners yesterday so you've got to come to the radio station and pick today's winner.'

Three hours sleep. Hung over, we get into the van and go to Richmond Hill to the radio station.

# The Krooked Cowboy

Larry has a tape of us on the radio station in Nashville singing *Happy Birthday* to me.

We did that and it was all fine and we picked the winner for that day. Afterwards, I was feeling better. I decided I might as well go back to school. Didn't do too much at Humber College except have a nap in the foyer.

Another time I went with Larry to the bluegrass awards in Nashville. His hotel was $100 U.S. a night and we could only afford to stay there a couple of nights. I ordered some orange juice through room service and it was $8 a glass and $22 a pitcher.

We checked out of there very quickly because our bankroll was getting pretty low and we moved downtown and across the river and got a room at the Interstate Inn, right off the Interstate. It was $100 a week – more our speed.

It was amazing how much was crammed into the day trip to Nashville . . . and what a bonus meeting Eddie Arnold.

The girls who were in the rooms next to us worked at a bar downtown and I think they were topless dancers, or waitresses. They were trying to get us to come to visit them at work, but we didn't have time for that. We were there to play music.

We stayed in that hotel one week. One morning I was standing on the balcony on the third floor, leaning against the railing, watching the sun coming up.

There was a bus parked on the side street. The door opened and this guy stepped off the bus and he stretched and yawned and put his hand over his eyes and looked up at me. He waved and he said, "Hi, Shawn, how are you doing." It was a fiddle player from Gananouque. He had come down to play some

**Shawn Brush**

When you're a Bluegrass fan, Bill Monroe is the man. Shawn got to meet him at the festival in Carlisle.

bluegrass in Nashville. They just pulled in there, driving all night, stopped there for some rest. When he got up in the morning I was the first person he saw.

Another time I went with the bluegrass club on a chartered bus to the SPBGMA (Society for the Preservation of Bluegrass Music of America) Awards in Nashville. Tony De Boer organized the trip and we stayed at a hotel near the airport in Nashville.

I joined the trip on the spur of the moment. Larry said to me, "Do you want to go to Nashville?"

"Yeah, when are we going?"

"In about an hour."

My mom and dad were on vacation in Florida, so I hopped on the bus to Nashville for the weekend. Barely slept that weekend.

My mom and dad were coming home on the Sunday, so I phoned from Nashville and my mom said, "Where are you?"

"I'm in Nashville."

I could have held the phone three feet away and she yelled. "What? When are you coming home?"

I got out of college in 1990 and was pretty set that I was not going to go back. I didn't feel there was anything there for me. Didn't know what I wanted to do. Didn't feel there was much for me to do.

Couldn't just go and work in a gas station, could just go and get a labour job. And the education side had this underlying tone, so I thought I would just have a good time for a while. Party and play some music and go to Bluegrass festivals. And so that's what I did.

Now this is where things get interesting too. Larry Sinai was like a constant companion to me. He had a car. Larry's older than me, of course, and he had a lot of friends in the bluegrass and country music.

Larry plays guitar and the fiddle and I love him a lot. He is family to me. He is a very unique fiddle player and he is a good bass player. I wish he would play bass more. He sings very uniquely, knows lots of songs and knows how to have a good time.

Shawn has visited the children's ward in local hospitals to entertain the youngsters.

# 12

# I want to be a songwriter

After winning the bluegrass award in 1991 and doing a demo with John Lewis, a guitarist with Ronnie Hawkins in the 80s, I started thinking there might be something for me careerwise writing songs.

I started going to little seminars in Toronto on how to get into the music business.

The independent artists scene was just getting going at that time.

It was in its infancy. It wasn't a big thing yet. This was the early 90s. At one of these seminars I picked up the name of a bar owner on the other side of Toronto, in a place called Newcastle/Bowmanville. I heard he had some songs on radio in Europe and was doing okay. Looked like he was good guy to talk to because he was doing what I wanted to do.

I jumped in the car in the summer of '91 and I drove down there and went into his bar on open mike night. There were a bunch of locals playing. I talked to him a little bit and said I was looking at getting my songs played on radio. I didn't have any money. I said I had won the bluegrass award. I was not looking at being a singer or a performer at that time, I just wanted to be a songwriter.

He didn't take me too seriously until I got up and sang a song at the open mike, accompanying myself on guitar.

## Shawn Brush

Everybody perked right up and listened and I have to admit that I was pretty naïve. I didn't think I was very good.

So this guy said, 'Hey, I want to talk to you.' We went into his office in the back of the bar and he said he could help me to get my songs out.

So he saw the dollar signs. But something told me I had better think about this and I said I would call him. So I went out to my car. I was tired because I had driven out there early. And it is a long drive from Burlington to Bowmanville and back. It may not be for you, but it is exhausting for me. It is about 120 kilometres each way, about an hour's drive each way.

I went down to a nearby truck stop, had a snack and lay in the car and slept for a couple of hours before driving back home. The next day I was convinced I made the right decision. I am sure he would have put my songs out there, but I don't think I would have seen much cash come out of it. You know how you get those kind of feelings when you want something really badly, but there is a voice inside saying 'slow down, don't rush into this.'

So I started investigating other things and at one of the seminars at the Royal York in Toronto I met Joe Wood, from Richmond Hill.

Murray McLaughlin, who did *The Farmer's Song*, was there talking to us and so was a guy named Ron Hynes, who was a great singer-song-writer from Newfoundland. He wrote a song called *Sonny's Dream* which is a great Canadian folk song that has gone around the world and been translated to many languages. He is another one of Canada's great exports of songs and songwriters and he was at the Royal York that day doing a guest speaking appearance.

I went down to the lobby on break and there was a guy named Richard Flohil, who runs a public relations firm, with clients such as the Canadian Country Music Association and the Mariposa Folk Festival. I met him, talked to him, and I was happy to be mingling in the right crowd. I went back up to the seminars and Murray McLaughlin did his speech on songwriting and Ron Hynes did his talk and spoke of the beginnings of the independent music business.

Back then the indie music business had the same kind of reputation as the self-publishing business. Common perception back then – and I am only talking about 18, 19 years ago – was if you were any good then a record company would sign you, you would become a big star, sell lots of records.

Making your own recordings, cassettes, was looked at, I suppose, like the self-publishing industry's vanity press.

# The Krooked Cowboy

But the recording industry, much like the book publishing industry, has been opened up to the masses by technology that lets you create a recording right from a computer in your own home and with a sound quality as good as, if not much better than the sounds that used to come from the huge recording studios of old.

Now it is pretty common for musicians to be indies, as they are called. Independent artists back then, when I was attending those seminars in Toronto, were looked at with a less professional eye.

I didn't get a chance to talk to Murray McLaughlin that day, but I remember coming out of the seminar and people were crowding around him. He was blocking the exit and I had to get on the GO Train. I was pushing my way through the crowd. I got up to where Murray was talking to his fans, signing autographs, and he looked down and saw me and I guess he thought I was coming up to talk to him. I looked at him, and I said, 'Excuse me, you are in my way.' He smiled and stepped aside to let me through. I think he got a laugh out of it. I just wanted to get to Union Station, get on the train and go back to Burlington.

I did get a chance to talk to Ron Hynes and I have met him a few times since. One time I gave him my *Wooden Hill* tape and also had the privilege of opening for him at the Mermaid Lounge in Hamilton.

Richard Flohil who has been one of the big names in the Canadian music scene for years, was also giving advice at one of these seminars.

It was summer of 1993 and I felt really good about myself. It was the first time for a long time that I felt really positive about myself. I bought some books and just lay out in the yard and read and rested. I started thinking of some new directions to take and a long term plan that I would become some kind of professional and do things that I had thought of doing.

I went to McMaster University in Hamilton and I talked to a couple of professors and they gave me some really good insight. I was looking at a 10-year plan - going to school for four years and get my BA and then go back to university for another couple of years and take a specialized course in – something! Lawyer. Teacher. Accountant. They all crossed my mind.

Another professor said you know what you should really do is go over to the disability office and talk to them about signing up and getting your classes organized and this was a good time to do it. It was the beginning of summer and I still had a lot of time before classes started in September.

## Shawn Brush

I found out where the disability office was on the McMaster University campus and I walked into that office and there was a guy in a wheelchair and a girl on crutches and a deaf guy. There was another guy who was blind. He could read one letter at a time with the help of special glasses. He was the guy I had an appointment to see. What happened in that conversation was something that altered my life.

I asked about getting funding to go to school. He said there were no grants available anymore, not even for disabled students. Handicapped individuals.

But he said the student loan programs give you the money to go to school and at the end of the schooling they usually write it off because they don't think anyone is going to be able to do anything to pay it off, or you are not going to live long enough. Now, these were his words, not mine.

I looked at him and I said, "Did you go to school here?"

"Yes."

"Now you work here?"

"Yes."

"Thanks. That's all I need to know."

I didn't want to be around that mental attitude, or anything to do with that kind of thinking at all. I was not interested in welfare or getting an education and a job just because I was disabled.

I had bigger dreams for me than sitting in a university knowing that the officials at the university and the government thought I was only there because I had a disability.

He said more in those few words, in that interview that lasted just a few minutes, than others who were giving me advice about my life over the years. And I had many, all of them, I am sure in their own way, wanting the best for me. Things like:

"Why don't you think about taking computers?"

"Have you thought about taking accounting?"

"You have to work really hard you know. It is going to be tough."

Everyone keeps telling me how hard it is going to be. Even learning how to drive, I was told, "Well, it is going to be really hard."

"You can't go to live on your own. You can barely take care of yourself."

108

# The Krooked Cowboy

All the things were said in good faith. And let me say that I emphatically believe that those who were giving me advice were thinking of the best for me. But because none of them knew me – I mean really knew me – I looked at their advice as being condescending goodwill at best. Simply, they didn't know me. My dreams are not based on my condition. I want to excel at all I do. I don't want sympathy. I am obviously governed by my size, my strength, my energy and my health. But I test them all to the limit as I go through life.

My body sets my limits on an ongoing basis. I don't let my mind set the limits. If I lived life the way others who love me and care for me would have me live, I would lose my independence. I would have a life that would be bounded by four walls.

I have managed to escape the institutional thinking. I have cracked the mould. I want to show other people who are like me that there is a life for us. We just need to be able to follow our dreams. I hope I am making sense . . .

# Shawn Brush

Shawn loves the outdoors - he often went fishing and hunting with his dad.

# 13

# First *Wooden Hill* cassettes sell out very quickly

I had just done my *Wooden Hill* demo. I got my cassette a few weeks later and now I wanted to start singing to promote it.

My first gig was a Wednesday night between Christmas and New Year's. I had 100 cassettes made in November and I sold them all before Christmas. Every single one of them.

Then I played a little gig and decided to get 1,000 cassettes of *Wooden Hill* made and do it up all professionally. I borrowed some money from my mother to make the second batch of the *Wooden Hill* cassette.

I was going to the Hamilton Folk Club and one of the guys there, Mark McNeill, who wrote editorials for the Hamilton Spectator, asked me if I wanted to see a story about me in The Spectator.

I said, "Sure."

The one thing I didn't want was any of the sympathy or the focus to be on my condition, I wanted my music to be the story. Paul Wilson did a human interest story and I thought that for the first story I would let that happen. I didn't just want to be a novelty. He did a really good job and I think it was presented well. It was not so much about the novelty as about the music.

## Shawn Brush

Then my cassette came out and I got into the music section of the Hamilton Spectator and I got into the  section called Now, not to be confused with Now Magazine in Toronto. They did a good review and story on me and I started getting comments. It was great press for somebody right out of the gate and I was doing everything on my own, from start to finish, pretty much.

It seemed I was very busy at that point.

I would get up early to drive my mom to work, so I could have the car. Mail some cassettes, get on the phone, have an afternoon nap, pick up my mom from work, drive to a gig, play the gig, pack up and come home and get up the next day and start it all over again.

After a while it just fizzled out. I just couldn't do it. No matter how much I wanted it to work out, I just was not physically able to do it. Determination and want are not the keys to success for someone like  myself. If you don't have the energy and the health, abilities can be severely restricted.

You gain a fan base and make your show known to be of such a high quality that people want to come to see you play. They know they will enjoy it. They buy your new recordings without even hearing the music because they know it is going to be good and they support whatever you do.

My first official gig was playing pedal steel guitar on a Saturday night at the Queen's Hotel in Dunville. I could not even carry a pedal steel guitar. The one I had at the time was a Fender 400. The frame is made of steel and it is much too heavy for me to carry so somebody always has to lug it around for me. My dad bought a pedal steel guitar from Eddie Fulawka, of Penetanguishene, the only guy in Canada at the the time who makes them. It came with a hand made case, but it still didn't make it any easier for me to handle. In time, I started putting rollers and casters on my equipment so that I could wheel it about. But this was the early days, I was just starting.

We get set up and start playing. A couple of our neighbours and friends followed us down to support the band, called Timberline. It turned out to be a night to remember.

A very big woman with tattoos from her chin to her ankles to her wrists decided she wanted to dance with me. She looked like a tough girl, but she seemed nice.  Not my type, mind you, but you don't get a chance to pick your fans, however you sure appreciate them all. I am not a dancer, never have been. As you can imagine it is not easy for me to find a suitable dance partner, and that stress on the legs doesn't do anything to quell the pain.

Shawn was Vice-President of the Skyway Bluegrass Club when he was the youngest member of Timberline. Others in the group are Bill Cymbala, Jerry Johnson, Ian Taylor and Art Wanders.

While I was playing she was on the dance floor and she kept smiling at me. I took a break and she came over to talk. She asked me to dance. I said I couldn't dance.

She kept bugging me and I must admit I was getting a little scared. Not that she would do anything intentionally to hurt me, but I just felt that she was encroaching, unnecessarily in my space.

She'd go away, then come back again and say, 'Oh, you're so cute' and 'I want to dance with you.'

We went up to play another set, and after it was over she was back at my table and all over me. I look at my neighbour, Debbie, and I say, "Have you met my wife?"

The tattooed lady said, "Oh, I'm so sorry. I didn't know you were married."

# Shawn Brush

She was so apologetic and started talking to my 'wife' who was sitting there with a big grin on her face.

Debbie looks at her and says, "You know what? It's okay, we have a very open relationship. If you want to dance with him, you can go ahead and dance with him." Everybody got the joke, except me and the tattooed lady.

Well, she picked me right up out of my chair, literally swept me off my feet, and carried me out to the dance floor. I didn't have a choice in the matter.

That was my first experience playing in a rock 'n roll band. I was still going to school. The goal of the band was focused around Art Wanders who was going to quit his job, we'd all go on the road and make some money.

We wanted to be successful enough that we could do it as a full-time job. It was so handy for me because Art was right across the street from me. He had a soundproof basement and I could put the guitar on a dolly and wheel it over there to practice whenever I wanted.

We had a really good drummer and I was lucky to be in a band with a drummer of that calibre at that time. He was a big asset to the band. He was a salesman in his day job, but wanted to give that up and go full-time with music. These guys had made a serious commitment to the band. We were practicing twice a week, at Art's house. I doubled on acoustic guitar and pedal steel. We'd run through some songs.

After two or three months we went to Kitchener. The country music radio station had a contest for bands. We thought it was a good idea to put our name, Timberline, out there, especially if we were serious about going full-time.

It was now the spring of 1991 and we got into the Sound of Music Festival in our hometown of Burlington.

We'd been practicing for six months. We were better than we needed to be. We knew it. There was one night we looked at each other and we knew we were good.

Art kept us at it, but we cut the practices back to once a week because we thought we had it down pat.

We went to the Sound of Music Festival and we were really good. The crowd seemed to like us. We felt we were getting ready for the road. We came off the stage in Burlington that really hot, humid summer day, and felt that it was just going to be a matter of time before we were going to get right into the music business.

## The Krooked Cowboy

Art picked his moment, gathered us around and said "I got us another gig." We were so excited. We all thought that this was it. Here we go. Look out Nashville, we're on our way

We were so excited I think we all asked the same questions at the same time - "Where? When?"

"It's the Christmas party at my work," said Art. Talk about a let down. Well, within about a week we all quit. It was such a big downer.

# Shawn Brush

Shawn has been fascinated by the Dreamcatchers made by Nick Huarde . . . and uses one as a backdrop at his concerts.

## 14

# Head over heels
# for a red-head

The summer of 1996 was looking pretty good. My back was acting up, but what else is new?

It was a Friday night, June 28, I remember it well because my niece Annie was born the next day. My sister Michelle was having her second baby. I was down at the Brant Street Station having nothing stronger than a ginger ale. I had thought about a beer, but my back was sore and I was taking some pills and I didn't want to do anything that would create a reaction.

I was sitting on a bar stool and I was pushing the chair back on its two back legs.

There was a stunning red-headed girl on the dance floor and I was having to lean back to see her because the bar was in the way.

So I pushed the chair back and I was sitting there quite comfortably drinking my ginger ale, admiring the girl. Not a care in the world. All of a sudden the legs on the stool slipped and went out from under me and I went straight down.

It was a really high bar stool. It was a tiled floor over the concrete. Carpet would have been a little better.

I landed right on my tailbone and back. I went down really hard.

I went down with such a clatter that people jumped up from their seats to see what had happened.

# Shawn Brush

A couple of people saw it happen and they ran over and went to pick me up, but I said, "Don't move me."

"Please don't touch me." I had learned my lesson when I broke my leg, someone thought I just had a charley-horse. Because I am small, people think I am like a child. But I am not. I may be the size of a child, but my bones are that of an old man.

If a child fell off a chair you would go to help them and more than likely pick them up. But you would never think of moving an old man.

I laid there for a good minute and for the first half of that minute I was probably paralyzed. I was numb.

I didn't move and I made sure they didn't touch me or pick me up. After about a minute I moved my legs and they pulled the chair out from where it had fallen under my legs. I laid there with my legs straight and I felt okay and I got up. By this time there is a crowd of people around.

I said I was okay, I did not need an ambulance. I would go home and lie down.

So I drove myself home and I went to bed. Next morning I went to hospital to see my sister who was there having her baby.

I had a bottle of painkillers and I was taking them. Lots of them. I am not one who likes to take pills, but the pain was unbelievable. I took the maximum dosage. I didn't make a big deal of it at the hospital. This was Michelle's day. I didn't want to take the spotlight away from her.

But everybody was asking me whether I was okay. I was having trouble walking. I told them I had hurt myself falling down. I didn't give them any details.

It is just a common thing.

People would ask, 'How are you doing?'

I would tell them my back is sore.

Then they'd say, 'Your back is always sore.'

I'd say, 'Yeah, I'm handling it.'

I was there to see my sister and the newest member of our family, her new baby.

Even though the pain in my back was killing me and I was right there in the

# The Krooked Cowboy

hospital, I never bothered to go to the doctor. I thought I was okay.

The next couple of days I just rested and took things easy. I thought I had just put a kink in it and it was out of place. I will be okay.

I looked back to the time I was a kid and the doctor who did the surgery on my legs. He perfected the back surgery, with the Harrington rod.

They used to do a procedure for curvature of the back – it's called scoliosis, curvature of the spine – where they would straighten the scoliosis by putting some metal rods in your back. Recovery took a long time – in some cases up to a year.

The doctor wanted to make that a quicker, better operation and he struggled with it for a long time. His son was going to school for engineering and was home doing some studying and told his dad he was bored,

His dad was working on the project – and then it occurred to him to let his son have a look at the problem.

The son took an engineering view of the situation, looked at it three-dimensionally and figured out within a couple of hours how to do these bars and place them in the spine.

He took it to his dad and his dad perfected this operation and patients could literally get up from the operating table and walk away from it.

The recovery time was very short compared to the previous procedure.

They looked at my back when I was about 14 and they wouldn't operate on my back because it was a mess.

So with this information, knowing that there was nothing that anyone could do to fix my back, whenever my back started bothering me I just put up with the pain. It will still hurt tomorrow, but maybe it will not hurt as much as it does today. No sense worrying about it and looking for a doctor to fix it. One of the best doctors told me as a young teenager that nothing could be done.

Then I fell off the bar stool.

I was supposed to play in the Home County Folk Festival.

My back was hurting. It was really excruciatingly sore.

I didn't let the pain keep me from playing music.

Andrea Lake was working on a record and she asked me to come and play guitar on a recording session and it was at Glen Marshall's studio in the north end of Hamilton. The studio was on the second floor and the live room was on the third floor.

Dan Achen from the Junk House band was producing Andrea.

It had been about two weeks since I had fallen. But they asked me to come in for 7 p.m. to do the recording session. About 4 o'clock I got up and started getting my stuff together to get ready to go. I stopped at Tim Hortons to get a ham and cheese sandwich and a drink. I started driving there about 5:30. I wanted to get there with enough time to get set up and be ready to go at 7. I always like being prompt.

I had to pull over because my back was just so sore.

I pulled over onto the side of the road and laid in the back seat. It was just so painful. I had a tear roll down the side of my eye.

I knew that something was wrong. It had been two weeks now.

Then my cell phone started ringing and I knew it was them at the studio because I had laid there so long. I sat up and ate my sandwich and I started to feel a little better. I took another pill.

I got in the front seat and drove to the studio, Andrea was sitting in the front waiting for me and was mad.

I said I was sorry I was late and explained that my back had been bugging me.

She stormed off up the stairs saying something like, 'I am paying for this studio time and you are late.'

I got in there. The guys in the studio didn't care. They had things to do.

Now I am there let's do it. I asked someone to carry my guitar and we walked up the stairs.

We got ready to do the song and then went up to the next floor in the attic and I sat there and played guitar and Andrea sang live from the second floor and they laid it right down to tape. Then they asked me to do a few more tracks.

We really worked on it for a few more hours and there was a song Andrea had written and she asked me to write the music for it a few weeks earlier so we laid that one down. It was two songs, but I did about five or six guitar tracks, all different kinds of versions and leads and rhythms and about midnight I came down and took a break and came in to hear the tracks.

# The Krooked Cowboy

The producer wasn't there. They told me Dan had got over me being late and had been inspired by my playing. He had gone home to pick up a 12-string guitar which he wanted me to play.

He asked me if I would. I said I would and we went on to the wee hours of the morning and I laid down five, six or seven guitar tracks, 12-string, six-string, and they were really pleased with it. One song made it on the record, one song didn't.

I came out of that session and I went home and lay down and stayed in bed much of the weekend. I knew something was wrong with my back and so I finally got up and went to my family doctor.

One good thing about always being in pain is that you never have to make an appointment with the doctor. I just walked in to my doctor. He had laryngitis and couldn't talk. I said my back had been really sore and so he ordered an x-ray.

When I returned to my doctor's office after having the x-ray done the secretary asked me if I could come back tomorrow (Tuesday) afternoon.

So I went back Tuesday and the doctor could not see me because the laryngitis was so bad, but he wrote me a letter and the secretary and the nurse gave me my x-rays and said, "You have got five compressed vertebrae. You have fractured all five of your lumbar" and he wanted me to see a surgeon right away.

He put a call in to see a surgeon and the closest appointment I could get was into August 1st.

I wasn't going to go and play. I phoned the guy in London and said, "I am not going to make it for the Home County Folk Festival." It was about two weeks away.

He said, "W-h-a-t?"

I said. "Well, I broke my back about two weeks ago."

He said, "Oh, that's okay." He understood. He managed to get Dave Talbot to take my place. Dave now plays with Dolly Parton's band.

When I went to see the specialist in Burlington, my mom and dad went with me. I walked into the doctor's office and I sat down in the examining room.

The doctor came and asked how I got there.

I said. "We drove."

## Shawn Brush

He said, 'No, How did you get in the building?'

I said. 'We parked in the back and we came in.'

He said, 'You walked?'

'Yeah.'

'According to these x-rays you should not be able to walk.' But he had really terrible bedside manner. He was not talking to me. He was talking to my mom and dad.

It was one of those times in my life where . . . here's a doctor . . . it takes a pretty high level of intelligence to be a doctor ... to be a surgeon . . . and he's treating me like a kid. A little kid.

He is not talking to me. I am 25 or 26 years old, but he is talking to my mom and dad like I am not there.

I bit my tongue, but he said there was nothing he could do and he referred me to a doctor in Hamilton at McMaster, who was a specialist of some kind.

I was still scheduled to play the Festival of Friends in August. I was going on the stage at noon on Friday, Aug. 10 and then at 4 p.m. and then the main stage on the Sunday at noon.

So it was a pretty good gig for me and I wasn't going to pass it up.

It had been about six weeks since I had hurt myself and the doctor I was referred to at McMaster, could see me on Aug. 10 at 11 a.m.

I was scheduled to go on at noon at the Festival of Friends.

My mom and dad drove me to Hamilton to see the doctor and he looked at my x-rays. He had the same bedside manner as the last doctor I saw, where it was like I was not in the room as he was talking to my mom and dad.

This time, I got really pissed off and I said something to him. He was really taken aback and my dad had to say to him, 'Look, he is a 25 year old man and he is right in front of you and you are talking about him like he's a kid, or like he is not here.'

He started talking to me. He said, 'Your back, even if it was in better shape, I wouldn't know where to start, there is so much wrong. I would be afraid to do anything.'

So that was the end of it.

Nothing was going to be done.

# The Krooked Cowboy

'Here's a prescription for painkillers.'

'Away you go.'

We left there and got to the Festival of Friends. I was a few minutes late, but I got on stage and played, broken back and all. Then went to lie down in the car until my next show at 4 o'clock.

I went on stage at 4, played. Came off stage, got back into the car, laid down in the back seat and my dad drove me back to Burlington.

Did the same on the Sunday, so I fulfilled my obligations that weekend.

August was pretty quiet and slow and I was feeling pretty down. But I managed to get out once in a while and do a couple of gigs. I took it easy and went at my own pace. But I was starting to take a lot of pills. I was taking them like M & Ms.

I started thinking, "What am I going to do?"

I'd still been writing songs

I had a bunch of new songs.

I had the *Land of Giants* CD.

I am thinking I'd like to get in and record, but it is getting too hard to play and what am I going to do?

It was about that time I wandered into a place called the Carrigan Arms, a pub right around the corner from my house.

It used to be called the Rusty Nail. I had played in there when I was 14, learning the blues from Jim 'Guitar' Avon.

There was a guy playing that night when I went in. His name was John Ludgate. He played guitar and sang. He also played a harmonica and he had a harmony machine. I had the pleasure of producing a casssette tape for John called *The Waves*.

He was playing his own versions of cover songs, as well as his own songs. I talked to him and got to know him. And right away I knew I wanted to produce a record for him.

I looked into a new avenue for me. Maybe I could produce and be a studio musician. I'd been playing in the studio for Andrea and Ray and a few other people. I had done a couple of other things here and there.

# Shawn Brush

We made a deal that I was going to produce a record for him. He was on a low budget and it was up to me to figure out how he was going to do it. It ended up that we recorded about 14 songs in one day with two acoustic guitars, bass guitar, electric lead guitar, harmonica, his vocals, and his harmony machine.

He had a machine that he sang through that it would make background harmony vocals when he sang. So we did it all direct and we did him live recording. Then him and I playing guitar. Then we laid down the bass and the electric guitar and we did it all in one day on a Saturday and I got really psyched up. He was recording and I sat beside him and I had a little drink and I had my Tylenol pills and every once in a while I would take another pill just to get me through it.

We did that recording and John put out a cassette.

About the same time I ran into Dan Robichaud who was the cab driver who used to take me to grade school and gave me my first guitar lesson. He wanted to put down some of his own songs and he asked me to produce it. So it was kind of fitting. I told him I would help him do it and he called it *Phoney Dreams*. It was a learning process for me. I didn't make a lot of money off it. I wouldn't charge him because it was like payback for him taking time to teach me the guitar all those years ago.

We did it in the same studio where we did John's cassette. It was Atilla Turi's studio where I had recorded *Wooden Hill* and mixed and mastered *Land of Giants*.

We worked with an engineer, some of it was Atilla, and another guy from Toronto, Mark Peters. He was a freelance engineer and he brought his own gear with him. Really high end. He had been working at Metalworks, a big studio owned by Rick Emmett from Triumph. He had been working with people like Anne Murray, world class. He had a good knack for the studio. It was really good working with him and I worked it out so that I wasn't making a lot of money, but I got a little kick back from the studio for bringing in a little bit of business.

I could go in a couple of times and record some of my stuff. So that's what I did when I wasn't producing.

We did John Ludgate's recording in one day and then we went in and mixed it all in one day. So we did an album in two days.

There were some songs on there that were really good. And he put them out later on a CD.

# The Krooked Cowboy

It was about that time that my buddy Dave John, who had played bass on the *Land of Giants*, had me interested in cutting some new songs and we went into Atilla's studio and we laid some songs down. He knew a drummer. I was against drums coming from the roots of bluegrass, but he talked me into it, and I really liked the sound that we got, so we did some demos.

I was not playing out as much and the back was acting up. I was taking a lot of pills. I remember going to Andrea's birthday party and everybody was playing music and I could tell that I was taking too many pills. It was becoming habit forming. I was still in pain but it was slowing me down. I went back to the doctor and asked him to give me something other than codeine.

So I took Ibuprofen, a 600 milligram pill. It was like taking about four or five Advils at once. I could take as many as I needed and they didn't make me groggy.

I just had to make sure I ate something with them. But I found that although I was still taking all these things I was still pushing myself too hard and I still needed to back off.

My pain is not like a headache. You take a pill for a headache and the headache goes away.

When you are having a pain that is going to be constant and forever, if you mask it and go out and do the same thing, you are just making the pain worse.

So I started doing less and feeling better. When I had broken my back, one of the things the doctor had ordered was a bone scan. I found out I had really low bone density. If you see it on a graph, here's a 20 year-old person, a 32-year-old person, a 40, 50, 60, 70, 80 year-old, Well my bone density scan came back that I had the bone density of an 85-year-old man.

They suggested I go on some calcium pills, new drugs that were designed to build up bone and stop bone loss.

At the time there were only a couple of drugs available for me as a man because a lot of the drugs are designed for elderly women and have female hormones in them. So there were only a few choices of drugs for me and one was a synthetic drug. The way it worked is that you took a synthetic pill for two weeks and it would be in your system and then you took the calcium pill and it would somehow be driven in to the bone by the synthetic one. Then after about eight weeks you would repeat the process because the synthetic drug would only last so long.

That was something that would supposedly stop the bone loss and help build bone back.

The synthetic drugs are designed for elderly people and they don't know what the long-term effect is for people to be on them for 30 years of their life.

I had no record of my bone density before I broke my back, so I thought I am going to go off the pills and just see what happens without taking anything.

That's what I did. I stopped taking it.

The Krooked Cowboy has loved riding horses since he was a toddler.

Collage of friends over the years.

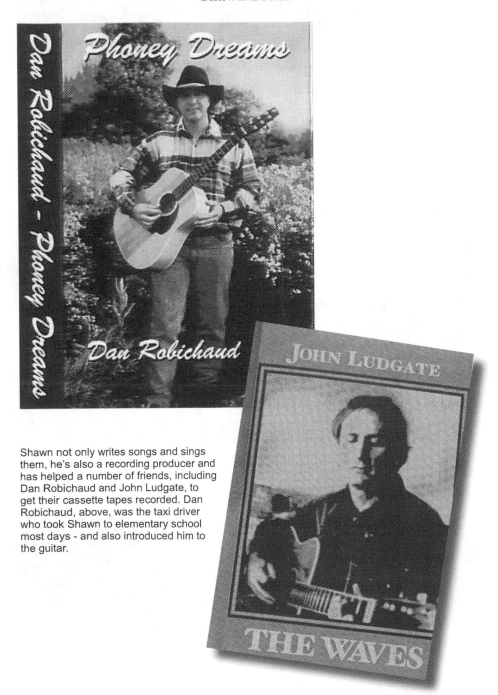

Shawn not only writes songs and sings them, he's also a recording producer and has helped a number of friends, including Dan Robichaud and John Ludgate, to get their cassette tapes recorded. Dan Robichaud, above, was the taxi driver who took Shawn to elementary school most days - and also introduced him to the guitar.

**15**

# Trying to get others to sing my songs

When I put a *Bootlegs* tape out I had received word that Daniel Lanois was recording a new album called *The Wrecking Ball* which he produced, as well as played and sang on it.

They were looking for songs and Ray Materick was sending a song and so was Tim Gibbons. I went to a music industry event on Barton Street and Tim Gibbons was there and was walking back up town, so I gave him a ride.

He said, "Dan really likes your *Wooden Hill* tape and he is going to produce Emmylou Harris. He asked if I had anything I could send down."

I got really excited. I gave him a tape, including one of my songs *Jacket and Jeans* which sounds like something Willie Nelson would sing,

He promised he was going to send something. I don't know if Dan or Emmylou ever got it. The music business is like that. You send things and nothing happens – or nothing appears to happen.

I know that it might appear that way when someone has gone to all the trouble to write a song, make a CD and offer it to someone to use as they see fit, that at least a little 'thanks but no thanks' note would be nice. But I guess the stars and their people get so many things sent to them they would need to hire extra staff to handle everything. So they just deal with those that they are going to use. When you think about it, it is no different than when a major corporation puts in an ad to hire an employee and says it will only respond to those who are chosen to be interviewed.

I don't get upset when I don't hear anything. I don't blame anyone. I don't suspect my work has not been passed along. I just accept that it was not suitable this time . . . and there will be another time.

# Shawn Brush

Word came down that Emmylou's record was a big success and Dan was going to produce Willie Nelson's next record and Brian Griffiths was going to play on it.

I was so excited that someone I knew was going to play with Willie Nelson. I couldn't sleep for three days I was so thrilled for Brian.

Tim Gibbons phoned and asked me for a copy of *Jacket and Jeans* because he wanted to give a copy to Willie Nelson.

I got a copy of the *Bootlegs* tape and I signed it to 'Willie from Shawn Brush.'

Go ahead, use one of my songs.

Tim phoned me and said he thought it was a great tape, especially that *Mizz Josephine*. He said he was going to do that himself.

I said, "Did you send it to Willie?" He said "No I am learning it."

He didn't send the tape. He kept it for himself.

I don't know if he ever did send it to Willie.

Tim did learn a couple of my songs and I learned *Whiskey Bar*, which I liked the first time I heard him sing it.

I was playing his songs and he was playing mine.

Tim was in L.A. and saw a guy who works with Daniel Lanois named Mark Howard. He is from Hamilton. I don't know him personally, but he's Dan's engineer and they were working on the soundtrack for Billy Bob Thornton's movie *Sling Blade*.

Of course, when it came out it was a big movie. It had Billy Bob Thornton, Dwight Yokum, John Ritter and a few other people.

Tim went down and he got a song in the movie called *Lonely Boy*. It is in the one scene with Billy Bob Thornton and John Ritter sitting in a café talking. It is way in the background, you can barely hear it, but, I believe, it was on the soundtrack album.

Mark Howard recorded an album for Tim. The movie came out and it took off and the soundtrack sold and people are asking, who is this Tim Gibbons guy?

He got a little bit of distribution with Glitterhouse Records in Germany and it got him another trip to L.A. to deal with a big publishing company, called Bug Publishing.

# The Krooked Cowboy

Tim said he was going to take my stuff down there to see if he could get anything going and he had been telling Billy Bob Thornton about me.

It was always great talking to Tim because he always had great stories.'

He told me he was playing on the radio in Arizona. He went on a tour to Texas. He was playing some of my songs when he was in concert, as well as on the radio. He told me that a couple of times he said, "You think I am great, listen to this," and he would play my song, *Michigan*. And he gave me credit for it.

He said the kids on Ventura Boulevard really liked my songs.

That was enough to pick a guy up and keep him going.

People tell me, 'Hey, I heard your song in Penticton, B.C.', or 'They really liked you in the Yukon.'

 I haven't been anywhere. I haven't toured.

This is coming to me from other people.

I look at this as another feather in my cap. Another notch in my belt.

But no money, of course.

The summer of 1998 had some highs and lows. I got some things conquered, yet the music thing was not taking off.

I was being played and discussed in the United States and other places around the world – even other parts of Canada – so I went to 820 CHAM, the local radio station in Hamilton and you'd think they would play someone local. Not on your life.

Then I started to see I had all these CDs sitting around. I had boxes of *The Wooden Hill*, boxes of the *Land of Giants*, couple of copies of the *Bootlegs* tape, boxes of the *Adrian Gail*.

I had a whole bunch of new songs I was writing, so I was getting frustrated. Understand that was 10 years ago. I have not mellowed. I still get frustrated – and I still don't get played on  local radio – but I can live with that. I don't look at my music being inferior, I just think those that play the music locally are not paid to play my music, or my music maybe doesn't fit into  their format. I have tried so many times to have my music played locally that I don't bother any more.  I have faith that one day they will want to play my music. At that point there will be no hard feelings – but there will be a happy singer/song-writer.

April 14 1997

Ontario Arts Council Jury
re grant application by Shawn Brush

Dear Jury:

You have before you a unique opportunity of supporting an artist of outstanding ability. Shawn Brush, despite his handicaps, has paid his dues and is a creator/performer of an exceptional calibre. In a couple of short years both, Shawn and his work have been in demand at festivals and workshops.

Do not support Shawn because of his condition. Judge him on his song writing ability, his guitar playing, and his incredible voice.

We know Shawn Brush well. From the first time he played at our coffee house, through bookings in the community and especially through his acceptance by peers at Festival of Friends, we knew he was a winner.

Shawn gives of himself 100% and volunteers for many benefits and fund-raisers.

Shawn is fiscally responsible, business oriented and always fulfills his commitments.

Do not hesitate to call for further information

Sincerely,
Hamilton Wentworth
CREATIVE ARTS INC.

*Bill Powell.*

William B. Powell
Executive Director

BN 10746-3499 RT
**HAMILTON WENTWORTH CREATIVE ARTS INC.**
401 Main Street West, Hamilton, Ontario, Canada, L8P 1K5
Telephone (905) 525-6644, Fax (905) 525-8292

# 16

# Ontario Arts Council became my *Anchor*

I set my goals on the Ontario Arts Council in 1997 because it was a grant more than loan. I understood there was a $10,000 limit for a recording session. The grant just covered 50 per cent of the costs of recording, not the printing and manufacturing.

I was dealing with Michael Shotton. He worked with me and helped me a lot.

We put our heads together and we picked out 10 songs to do a full length album.

We wrote up a budget and the grant proposal.

Michael had a few other projects he was working on.

He is a professional singer, plays drums, plays guitar left-handed/upside down, and he was from the north of England in Newcastle. He had a band called Vongroove. They were really popular in Japan and Europe, but just couldn't make it in Canada.

He would go on tour in Japan and girls would break into the hotel and mob them. They are a heavy metal/pop rock band.

When I first started hanging out on the Hamilton music scene in 1993, I knew

# Shawn Brush

Mike from his days playing jam sessions at O'Toole's.

I got to know Mike over the years so in 1997 we put in this proposal to do a professional high-end commercial record. We picked out the songs and sent in the proposal. Then it was a waiting period up to about six months to find out if you had it.

I kept to myself.

I think I maybe went to one or two bluegrass festivals, like Tottenham and the one on Highway 6 and played the odd gig. Kept writing songs. I was writing some songs with Mike.

Part of the grant proposal was that we had to demo three songs that were going to be used on the project.

We co-wrote one song called the *Anchor*. I wrote it after I heard a story on the radio about a fellow from New England who had written a book called *The Perfect Storm*.

It was based on a true story about a fishing boat, called the *Andrea Gail* which was caught in the worst storm in recorded history in the Atlantic Ocean. Three storm fronts collided and these guys were fishing the Grand Banks off Newfoundland in the North Atlantic. It was late September. They were on their way home and they were lost at sea. It was a story that really inspired me.

The book was all about these guys after losing radio contact and it talked about what might have happened. It was later made into a movie starring George Clooney. I had heard about this book and someone on the radio talking about it. It was one of those things that stuck with me. Fascinating story.

It was a neat take on reality.

I came up with the idea that it would be cool to write from the ship's point of view. What I did is I wrote a song called the *Anchor*.

I had written piles of verses and I really wanted to write a song that was kind of like Stan Rogers' stuff about the sea and the ships.

I had the story written and Mike Shotton came over to my place one night and we had a writing session and I told him about the idea.

He said that was kind of cool. It had a James Taylor vibe to it.

He is very, very musical and melodic and he was stretching my musical talents. We worked on it a long time. It was a long song.

We went in and did a demo of it and it was six or seven minutes long. We did a demo of another song and then did *Don't Give Me The Blues*.

I remember doing that at three in the morning. Acoustic guitar. Some keyboard. Me singing lead and Mike sang some harmony vocals behind it.

We did not re-record it because it was so good on its own. We went with what we had intended to be the demo.

We sent that in with the grant proposal and then we did the sit and wait thing to see what happens. We were waiting for the word to come back on the grant money from the Ontario Arts Council.

**Grant Avenue Studio**
1985 INC.

May 9, 1997

To Whom It May Concern:

This letter confirms my support for a recording project for Shawn Brush. I am familiar with Shawn's music; he being an active member of the Hamilton musical performance and recording scene.

Shawn's music is roots based, highlighting his considerable talent at writing both lyric and melody. On his 1995 CD recording, he delivered an excellent performance.

I would be pleased to work with Shawn and believe that he has the talent and marketability to warrant an investment in producing a second album.

If you require further information, please don't hesitate to contact me.

Sincerely,

Bob Doidge
Producer/Engineer - Grant Ave. Studio

bd/md

**Shawn Brush**

Shawn made the cover of Bluegrass Canada magazine in 1994.

**17**

# *Adrian Gail -*
# **The true story**

My 1998 CD was a success, even though I made a huge mistake. The CD was the *Adrian Gail*. I didn't check my facts and after everything was printed I discovered that it should have been called the *Andrea Gail*, after the fishing boat that was made famous by the blockbuster movie *The Perfect Storm*, starring George Clooney.

I could have been forgiven had I spelled Gail as Gale, seeing it was a big storm. But I have no excuses, just carelessness for Adrian rather than Andrea. Not too many ships are named after males. I should have known.

I am not the first artist to make this mistake on a CD and I probably won't be the last. I remember reading Stompin' Tom talking about his *Northland's Own* LP being changed to *Northlands Zone* when it was reprinted. No excuses, but I did learn a valuable lesson.

While I can write the songs, music and lyrics it is always a struggle to come up with the money to do all the technical aspects of the project. There is studio time, back-up musicians, master tapes to get done, you need a graphic artist to design the cover and then someone to do the CD packaging. It's not cheap. Neither is it easy to beg, borrow and steal.

I must have some of the best friends in the country, creative professionals willing to give their time and share their talents to help me. There have been times when the entire project was donated, or friends acted as my banker and spotted me the $1,000 or so that it takes to get a CD recorded and in circulation.

# Shawn Brush

The *Adrian Gail* was no exception. A Burlington graphic artist, who was also a fan of my music, helped design the cover and the CD packaging and we ended up using a picture that a friend of mine took.

We were on the Burlington beach strip one day and it was really storming. The waves were coming up on the beach by the lift bridge, so I stood out on the pier and the waves were crashing up behind me. I really liked these pictures and we used them on that cover. Barb found a picture of a fishing boat that was similar to the Andrea Gail.

I put out the CD after giving it a lot of effort and I managed to get 300 CDs made and they went pretty fast. I gave a few to each guy that played on it.

Because they went so quickly, I thought I had better order another 500 to 800, whatever I can get. So I did that and wouldn't you know it, sales just kind of stalled.

I was sending the CD to managers and I was getting some great reviews from the music critics, like 4.5 out of five for the quality and the songs and the music and the production. Everything was A-plus.

However, the radio guys were not picking up on it. *In the Land of Giants* CD when I put that out, all the folksy guys and guys that were playing me already played some of it, and the country and the bluegrass guys played what they could of it.

I took *Land of Giants* to 820 CHAM in Hamilton but they flatly refused to play it. Excuses included 'It is not commercial' and 'It is too much like old country.'

Haven't you got a Hank Williams hour – play the Hank Williams–type song?

But they wouldn't.

When I put out the *Bootlegs* tape the folk and the bluegrass guys were playing that and the radio guys in Dauphin, Manitoba and Newfoundland, Quebec, Nova Scotia, and British Columbia. The *Adrian Gail* got the same play from the same guys. I shouldn't forget to thank and mention Niagara Falls, and the Brock University Country Hour (in St. Catharines, Ontario), their singer/songwriter special, for always playing my music.

However, commercial radio hardly touched the *Adrian Gail*. It was practically non-existent. And I still owed the producer a pile of money for it. But that's the story of not only my life, but the life of most Indie recording artists in Canada.

# The Krooked Cowboy

It was back to square one. Back to the drawing board.

Another thing I wanted to say about radio air play is the feedback I was getting from the rural areas. There were a couple of guys who played banjo and guitar at the Skyway Bluegrass Country in Burlington. We used to meet at the Boilermakers in Hamilton and then Industrial Street in Burlington and later at the Navy Veterans Hall and they also had a workshop night on Thursdays in Waterdown.

The guitarist was Mike and his buddy Graham played banjo. They were hippie kind of guys, and they liked Neil Young and the Grateful Dead. Besides rock 'n' roll they also liked playing Bluegrass. They were both outdoorsy guys. One was going to school for fish and game to work as a ranger in the provincial parks and the other had a helicopter pilot's licence and a pilot's licence and he got a job working for a mining outfit in northern B.C. and the Yukon. He came back to Burlington after six months and he said he needed another *Wooden Hill* tape, because his had worn from too much playing.

He said he would go into the northern towns that were hundreds of miles apart and instead of a juke box in the bars they all had a ghetto blaster with a tape deck. He was sitting in one club up there in northern British Columbia and he gave them the *Wooden Hill* tape to play on the ghetto blaster.

They had one of those tape machines with the dual decks so they could make a copy of it for the bar.

He went back to work and took his tape with him and he came back a couple of weeks later and they were still listening to the tape.

At another bar they were playing *Wooden Hill*.

It was a copy of a copy and there were about 25 copies of the copy around.

I knew I had a following of people out there, people enjoyed my music.

The *Adrian Gail* was so different from anything else I had recorded. And it was slick and professional but it really wasn't being accepted by the mainstream. The songs were a bit too long and maybe they weren't as upbeat and dancing type of songs, but I was getting respect for my work. But no royalties.

When the royalty cheque finally came in for the Adrian *Gail* it topped out at $65. And that's what I made when I did the RDR (Rosedale Records) CD. It cost me $1,000 to do the RDR and it cost me way more to do the *Adrian Gail*.

# Shawn Brush

Shawn leads a hectic life . . . always pushing himself to do something new - or more. Often he pays the penalty for his exhuberance . . . and has to take things easy for a few days. But then he's back at it . . . making a name for himself as a talented and accomplished musician, singer and songwriter, who loves to produce his own recordings and shares his technical skills with others trying to break into the entertainment business.

## 18

# The $5,000 wheelchair!

Getting a wheelchair isn't that easy. The government just doesn't like to part with funds. When I look at all the waste that goes on with public funds at all levels of government it never ceases to amaze me how people have to dance through hoops to get what I would consider the necessities of life.

I was pretty low on funds.

I had borrowed money from my sister to put the *Land of Giants* CD out and I had to pay her back. I had paid the studio off for the studio time. I had some phone bills.

Little things here and there, but it was adding up. Driving a car. Gas.

In order to get the funding for the ADP (Assisted Devices Program) for the wheelchair they had to send out a physical assessment person to the house to see me.

They take a look at you and your circumstances and they decide what they think is best for you.

They say if you can't get out of bed to go to the washroom or get to the kitchen to get something to eat, that you need a wheelchair and that it is only for use in the house.

# Shawn Brush

It is not for lifestyle. It is for basic need.

I could walk, but yet I was in pain, especially when I first got up in the morning, or depending on what I did during the day. So I was on this borderline. They told me that I don't really need a wheelchair, and that I could get by with canes or a walker.

It took a lot of convincing, frustration and arguing with this physical therapist to say well you are not here to see me in the morning when I get out of bed. I was firm. I said I needed the wheelchair.

We have stairs in the house. How are you going to get from here to the kitchen.

They went out and the first thing they did was get me a walker. That really didn't work out because there are no walkers that were made to size for me. They are all made for people of average height. I needed something much smaller.

Eventually, she got a wheelchair and I had to show I could use the wheelchair up and down the stairs. Much like when I was in my cast I would sit on my rear end on the step, lift the wheelchair over me and put it onto the next level; or lift it down. I got a wheelchair with wheels that came off so I could manoeuvre much easier. I could put it in the car and take it with me.

Frankly, I was thinking more lifestyle so I could get out and do stuff without being in constant pain and run down.

So finally she saw that the best choice was to have a wheelchair.

We looked at all the different kinds of wheelchairs on the market. She was looking at the pedal car price, I was looking at the Cadillac. Why do civil servants handling these social service necessities look at cutting corners? I would love to get one of the assessors that hands out hundreds of thousands of dollars to artists and artisans to make one of their weird dreams become a reality. There seems to be no end of senseless waste in the arts area – projects that help no-one, other than line the pockets of the artist who had the gall to ask for the moon for something that ends up getting publicity all over, usually for the stupidity of the government in handing out these grants, rather than the arts value of the project.

I really have nothing against artists and artisans. In fact, I have a lot of praise for their interesting ways to expand creativity. My beef is just with the seemingly double standards of necessity. Helping someone to get about and become as useful as possible and not so much a hindrance on society, or a burden on family members, versus paying an able-bodied artist a hundred thousand dollars to paint a meadow green.

Enough on that.

Back to my quest for a wheelchair. I wanted to get something that was good on my back and because I was lifting the chair up and down the stairs, in and out of the house and in and out of the car, I needed something that was lightweight. Something that would support my back when I was in it.

The chair we finally looked at was called a Barracuda and it was made from lightweight aircraft aluminum, composites, carbon fibre and titanium. It was more of a sports chair. It was really light, really expensive.

I think it retailed at $5,000.

The ADP only covered so much – I think about $2,000 - and they had a backrest they suggested I get for my back. The ribs in it were adjustable to contour to your back.

It is lightweight and strong.

The back rest was designed by the guys who did engineering for Mercedes Benz.

March of Dimes usually helps fund wheelchairs, but they didn't know whether they could come through with the funding for this one.

I had some debts that needed to be cleared, so I didn't have any room on VISA or any other credit card.

Mom and Dad had talked about putting a shower in the basement where there was only a toilet and a sink.

With the wheelchair in the house I had to have something that was accessible – and that was the basement. So it was going to be a big cost to renovate.

I thought I needed a benefit concert so I asked all my friends and my mom went out and got some businesses to donate prizes and there was a club on Plains Road called the Hanging Tree. I was talking about having the benefit in 1997 for my wheelchair.

I asked everyone I knew to come out and play, Tim Gibbons, Ray Materick, Andrea Lake, Jennifer Flook (now known as Hunter Eves), Bert Steen, Mike Shotton and Dave Bata, a Rod Stewart impersonator.

# Shawn Brush

We had it on the Sunday night. Had the benefit. Got the money. Did the renovations in the house over the winter to put in the shower stall.

We got the letter back from Ontario Arts Council. They were going to give me the grant, but they didn't accept the $10,000 they were only going to give us $3,500. It turned out the grant was only 35 per cent on the total amount.

I had put on the thing that $10,000 was going to come out of my own pocket and from some investors and the way the Ontario Arts Council looks at it, if they are putting in $10,000 we will put in 50 per cent of what is adequate to do the recording.

Basically, we were making a record on $3,500. Mike and I talked about it and we decided we could do six songs - an EP - and the one demo that we sent in was *Don't Give Me The Blues*, and it was such a good demo we didn't have to rerecord it. So there was one song. We needed five more songs. We had to do the three songs we put into the proposal and then we could pick out the three other songs. I put 10 songs on the proposal, and part of the agreement was that we were going to record the 10 songs, or they could ask for their grant money back. This came down to me being ballsy, let's do the six songs, it is my name on it, I am the one taking the chance.

We started recording and it was the whole winter when we worked at night when Mike had a chance to do things. There were a few days when I had to get up early and go and do things with him. We recorded bass, drums, guitar, vocals, keyboards, pedal steel, mandolin, fiddle, Hammond organ, all separately, and Kevin Briggs came in separately and played guitar on a few tunes.

Mike had a session he was working on with a couple of people and there was a big studio in Richmond Hill, a million-dollar studio. They have floating floors and separate heating for the studio and all the equipment. They have all the different formats to record in and it is big enough to record an orchestra in.

We were going to do the bed tracks – the drums and the bass there – and some of my acoustic guitar. We did pre-production at Mike's house and then we went up to Richmond Hill and I was basically being a night person full-time at that point in my life. I went up there and ordered in some supper and sat in for the night to do these bed tracks because they worked all day doing the other session that Mike was working on.

I took the 407 and it ended right at Richmond Hill and got off and went to the studio. Did all the bed tracks and got out of there just after midnight. Got some good stuff and we started laying down the tracks and doing the recordings.

# The Krooked Cowboy

Finally, it was ready and I had to raise some funds to get the CD manufactured. Mike and I talked about all the costs and it ended up that I owed him money for his time in the studio and it was pretty substantial. He agreed to just get the record out and we will figure out payment later. Just pay me as you go, don't worry about it. Just get the record out. Get something happening. He gave me the name of a few managers and people to contact and he thought that something could happen with it. He had a stake in it. He had co-written a song on it. He was putting his name on it. Everything he touched he works hard on and he was putting in a 110 per cent effort. He doesn't let anything go until he is happy with it, which is a mark of professionalism. Even if you have to pay for it.

Shawn with Garth Hudson of The Band at the 2008 Hamilton Music Awards.

Kyle Weir photo

**19**

# The song that became a *Shadow* of myself

There are two songs I want to talk about right now. One day I was sitting after my car broke down in 1999. It was wintertime. It was cold and I was broke. People were hounding me for money, including the credit card company and I was sleeping all hours. My back was sore and life in general was like monotonous. I was just trying to make it through.

I remember looking down in my office. The light was shining and I could see my shadow on the ground.

I looked at the shadow and I started writing a song. The lyrics told the story of the *Shadow* coming to life and the *Shadow* was singing the song. There are a lot of people who will let you down in this life is my thinking, but once in a while there is someone who comes through.

Your shadow is always with you. Your shadow never leaves you. Your shadow is a part of who you are, kind of like the Peter Pan shadow and the shadow comes to life.

The *Shadow* sings the song and when I called it the *Shadow* I wrote the song for me.

# Shawn Brush

Somebody asked me at one time. "Who did you write that for?" And I never told anybody. But I wrote it for me when I was low. That picked me up again. It's a great song and it is really simple. I can see it going places, it doesn't matter who sings it.

I woke up early one morning – 8 or 9 o'clock, which is like the middle of the night for me – and I just couldn't go to sleep. Words were in my head and when I get them like that I run them through my head like a dialogue, like a tape machine, like a loop, they repeat over and over and if it is good it sticks. Then I write it down, and usually it goes away. This wasn't going away.

The whole song was there. All the words were there. Finally, I wanted to sleep but I couldn't because it was just going in my brain. I usually keep a pen and paper by my bed so that I can write. I still do that.

That night I didn't have a pen and paper. So I had to get out of bed and I went in the next room and got a pad of paper and I wrote down the words...

*Who's gonna love me  when I'm down and out*

*Who's going love me when I'm blue*

*Who's gonna hold me the whole night through.*

I wrote it verbatim. I didn't have to edit it. It just poured right out of me, the fastest song I ever wrote that way. It was done. It was out of my head, committed to paper.

I reached over and picked up my guitar and I played an E chord and I sang it. It just wrote itself.

It was like a gift.

It was one of those moments. I wrote the *Wooden Hill* and *Seasons* very easily, but *Who's Gonna Love Me* was finished as fast as I could write it and pick up the guitar it was written and it was in stone. It was done. It wasn't edited. It wasn't changed. The process was finished. The creative energy, wherever it came from.

20

# Opening for the stars

I have made a lot of friends in the music business. I have also had the honour of opening for a number of the acts - stars in their own right.

Fred Eaglesmith, Prairie Oyster, Natalie McMaster are some that come to mind. But there have been many others.

When I first started playing music live, I used to go to the club La Luna where singer-songwriters and up-and-coming acts, even folks touring from the states would come and play in Hamilton.

I had heard a lot about Fred Eaglesmith, from Port Dover, and when I found out he was going to be playing at La Luna, I went along to see him.

He was my kind of artist - he played guitar and sang, but also writes all his own stuff.

I went to see him for a couple of reasons. His reputation was good in the Hamilton area, and he had got into music the same way I had, playing bluegrass.

Fred had done a lot of bluegrass in the late 70s and early 80s for Tony DeBoer. Playing mandolin for Fred was Willie P. Bennett, who used to play in the Dixie Flyers in the 1970s and he was playing bluegrass and folk in the late 1960s and early 70s. Willie, who made many records in those days, died early in 2008 in Peterborough.

# Shawn Brush

Willie was a great singer-songwriter in his own right.

Also with Fred that night was Ray Pickersgill, playing dobro. He was also from Port Dover.

Ray was another musician I knew from the bluegrass days in the mid-80s when Carlisle, like many other places, had bluegrass festivals.

Usually, Washboard Hank played dobro with Fred, and Ralph Skipper, was the bass player. But this night Washboard and Skipper were not there.

It was a magical night. The place was packed. It was very acoustic. Very intimate.

Fred was awesome.

I gave him one of my *Wooden Hill* tapes. He had what he called a box set of his recordings - two cassettes in a homemade wooden box, I couldn't resist buying the box set and he autographed it for me. I still have it, in fact it is a bit of a collectors item because the labels on the tapes are wrong and the booklet that comes with it has some of the pages printed upside down.

Fred played two sets and at the end of the night Willie P. Bennett was sitting up there and he did one song and he just blew my mind. This guy was the best singer-songwriter I had seen in the flesh, besides Ray Materick.

It was an eerie song. I have a saying that I save for the best - Good is good. Great is better. He was great.

He totally floored me. He toured all over the world with Fred.

When I used to play Hamilton's Festival of Friends, I met up with Fred a couple of times. He was always good to talk to, a really good guy. He remembered getting my tape of the *Wooden Hill*. He said he listened to it and he liked it.

I was playing lots of little cafes in different places and trying to stay healthy and fit as well as I could be and there was a place out in Port Dover called Captain Billy's, a little neighbourhood bar across from the Norfolk Tavern.

I called Wado Texas, a rockabilly guy, one day to see if I could sing at Captain Billy's.

His family owned Captain Billy's and it ended up being one of my favourite places to play.

I opened for Natalie McMaster at the Lighthouse Theatre in 1996.

A few people knew me around Port Dover and the next time I played Captain

# The Krooked Cowboy

Billy's I phoned before I went to ask Wado if he and Fred were going to be in the audience that night. He was down in Nashville with Fred.

Just before I started playing Wado walked in the door with Jenny Whiteley and Fred Eaglesmsith.

Fred and Jenny sat down in the front of the restaurant and ordered some drinks. I talked to Wado for a minute and he said they were in Nashville where they played their gig. Jenny and Fred were in no hurry to get back, but when he told them Shawn Brush was playing they decided to drive home to see me. At least that's the way I heard it. That's the way I like to think it happened.

They all lived in Port Dover at the time.

They listened to me play all night.

Fred said, " Play the *Wooden Hill*.'

I played a whole bunch of my songs.

Fred said he really enjoyed it. There were only four or five people, but I played my heart out.

When I was taking a break, almost at the end of the night, Fred looked at me and said, "You are a great songwriter, man. I just came from Nashville you'd blow all them guys away."

It felt really good.

He said, "I want you to play in my festival next summer. You are the first guy hired. You are closing out Saturday night. You call the girl and tell her Fred said."

I said. "Thanks Fred."

"I am serious," he said.

He gave me the number of his manager and said it was a charity picnic, doesn't pay a lot of money but it is good exposure. People come from all over. They really listen to the music and they will buy the CDs.

I gave him a copy of all the CDs I had. He took them all.

He asked for more  to take to Nashville. Jenny Whiteley wanted some to take to Toronto.

Besides  playing his festival in 2000, Fred also invited me to open a few shows for him. One was in Toronto at a club called Ted's Wrecking Yard and the other was at Hamilton's La Luna. They were back-to-back nights. He was home for the Christmas holidays and had some shows to do around Ontario.

I went down to Toronto with a friend named Ron Robertson, better known as Cabbage. I got to know him when we both hung around the same music spots in Burlington. He has turned out to be a really good friend of mine. Ron has been playing music for years. He also writes songs.

He was a big fan of Fred Eaglesmith's and when I said I was going to open for Fred he jumped at the chance of driving me to Toronto for the show.

The club was up in the second floor so Cabbage carried my guitar for me.

My friend Bert Steen came down to check out Fred Eaglesmith and his band the Flying Squirrels.

I had been trying for years to get into Toronto to play. I couldn't break into that scene.

So here I was opening for Fred Eaglesmith – and with a full house.

I'd stop, sing a song and I'd finish and there was silence. Then when I finished the set, Fred was backstage and he said, "That was great man, they loved you."

After the show, Fred said, 'How did you do?'

'I sold two CDs.'

'You are doing better than me,' said Fred,

The next night was Friday in Hamilton. We had a good turnout.

In January 2000 I got a call from Fred Eaglesmith about a big show at the Air Canada Centre (ACC) for Canadian farmers, similar to Farm Aid in the U.S. where money is raised by performers to help farmers. A lot of Canadians are not aware that Farm Aid is a big thing in the States, but many Canadian farmers have it a lot worse, and struggle to make ends meet.

Fred Eaglesmith, who has a lot of respect for the farmer, grew up in a farming community. A lot of his songs are based around farming and rural Ontario.

He was one of the headliners at the Sunday convention.

The only problem was he was scheduled to play in St. Jacobs that same afternoon. He didn't want to turn down the event for farmers at ACC, so he asked me to open for him in St. Jacobs and play until he arrived.

# The Krooked Cowboy

The St. Jacobs gig was at a school house built in the 1860s. I didn't need a public address system because the acoustics were fabulous.

The crowd was there to listen to Fred do a solo show.

They were surprised when I showed up, but they understood that Fred would be there as soon as he could.

There were people who had driven from Ottawa that day to see Fred. Another had come in from Ann Arbor, Michigan. There were others from London, Windsor and Kitchener. My friend Chris Whelehan drove up from Toronto.

My friend Cabbage came. My mom and dad were there, too.

The place was full.

It was a good crowd and they were all there for the music. A nice January day in southern Ontario. I played for 45 minutes to an hour before Fred showed up.

Fred heard me do my last few songs. He told the crowd I had CDs and at the end of the show people came up and they bought the CDs.

Fred gave me a couple of bucks for playing, one of his t-shirts and a couple of CDs to take home.

He gave me one of his old LPs from the 80s. I was happy it was a successful day.

Later on that spring, Russell deCarle, the lead singer, and Keith Glass, of Prairier Oyster were hanging out in Hamilton and they wanted to do a gig at the Mermaid Lounge. I got asked to open for them.

The morning DJ from 820 CHAM introduced them and I opened the show and afterwards the DJ said to me, "Man, you are one great singer-songwriter and player."

'Yeah."

This is the same station who won't play my records.

He tells me if I am ever playing anywhere, to let him know. "I'll pump the hell out of it. Keep at it. Keep it up," he said.

It was summer and time for Fred's weekend festival. A very good friend of mine named Gordon Greig wanted to go to the festival with me. Got down there Friday night, got set up and checked in with Fred Eaglesmith.

## Shawn Brush

There was a good crowd there and I met Fred's wife, Mary, and his manager. They had both been out to see me play. Mary had a table set up with Fred's CDs, tapes and records, so I gave her two boxes of my CDs, *Steeltown* and the *Adrian Gail*.

We put them out on the table and after the last show finished at midnight, Gord and I went back to the cottage in Port Dover and we stayed up all night singing and playing.

I rested at the cottage and wrote a couple of songs that weekend. On the Saturday night I was to play.

We made supper and loaded up the van and drove to the festival. I was going on around 10 Saturday night. I was closing out the show.

It went really well. It was about 11:30 and I got an encore. I got another encore.

I said I will play all night if they let me. And I would have, too.

Fred came running up and said, "Play *The Wooden Hill.*'

I did.

Everybody loved it. Gord told me he was sitting in the audience and there were a couple of guys sitting behind him who couldn't see the whole stage. They were arguing about how good it sounded. One guy stood up and walked through the audience so he could see the other side of the stage. He came back and sat down beside his friend and he said, 'It is only one guy playing guitar.' They thought it was two guys playing because of the way I play.

Gord just laughed.

Sunday afternoon they had a big barbecue at the festival and we went back over. I went to check on the CD sales.

I had sold only one or two of the *Adrian Gail* – that's the one I spent about $10,000 producing it.

The *Steeltown* CD that I recorded at my friend's apartment on one microphone on the computer, and did everything really cheap. Just me and the guitar. I had sold 30 or more of those.

The thing is what they heard me play solo ... that's what they saw. That's what they heard. That's what they wanted. And that's what they bought.

That was the clincher for me. For me to invest any money in a big recording, that's a long shot in many ways. And especially right there at the CD sales table.

Things were winding down and there was Willie P. Bennett and he was going to be playing in Hamilton in October. I had opened for him previously in 1999.

Gord and I left the festival and came home. I had no gigs lined up for a couple of weeks until the guitar man Dave Essig was coming from Vancouver.

# Shawn Brush

Bob Lanois photo

Shawn with one of the models for the medicine show.

# 21

# Almost . . . a millionaire

When I was playing in Milton there was a guy who would come out and see me play. He was kind of a leather jacket and cowboy boots motorcycle guy. He had a Harley Davidson and his wife had a Harley Davidson and they would ride to come see me play. He was friends with my buddy Cabbage. In 2000 when the depression hit, Mark came to a birthday party. We sat down and I told him what I was going through, that I was fed up with everything. He said, "Well, have you ever thought about putting a business plan together? I'd love to help you out."

He would send me an email and ask me how I was doing, you know, what was happening. My friend Cabbage said to me, "Mark's pretty successful. He has money you know, he's a scientist, he's a businessman you know. You might want to talk to him, take his advice. You know, he'd like to help you." This was August of 2001. I got on the phone and I spoke to Mark and he said, "Well, what do you want to do?" I said, "Well, do you want to come down here? I don't know where you live." He said he lived in Georgetown. He came down this one summer night. We sat in the backyard. He said, "Have you got a plan?" I said, "Well, what do you want out of it? Why are you asking?" He said, "You're a tenacious guy. I'd like to help you. I'd like to see you make it and make a living and fend for yourself and all that." So he was talking the right language. I said "Well, ok let's do something." He said, "Well, decide what you want to do and come see me in a couple of weeks."

In the middle of August, I went up to Georgetown to see him. He had a Jaguar in the driveway. He had a big SUV truck. There were three motor homes.

He had a few other cars, a nice house, and nine, count 'em nine, Harley Davidson custom motorcycles.

We sat at his kitchen table. I came up with this idea of having a theatrical road show to play in theatres and go across North America. He said, "Great! Let's start working on it." A friend of his popped by to visit him and he was a successful business guy. I told him briefly what I wanted to do. They had some business to talk about and so they said we'd talk some more later. The next day I got an email and he said, "Me and my buddy could put $100,000 into it. You can use the motor home and get started and we can put this together. First thing we need to do is have another meeting next week and I want you to come back up to my house."

So I went back up there the next week. I was excited and I stopped to get gas on Highway 5. I only had $20 in my pocket so I put in $20 cash to get to Georgetown.

I told him in a nutshell how I wanted it to be and he said he'd get a writer to write it and 'get it out of your head.' I'd have to explain everything in detail and we'd get an artist to draw the pictures so we can see what you want to do and you'll have to work with the artist. I said "Ok, great!"

All that day, I was on a high, you know. It meant I was finally getting a break.

The fellow who wanted to help me was in the business of nanotechnology. His company had a number of offices throughout Toronto, with a lot of projects with the University of Toronto.

He was a pretty smart guy. I went to his house and he showed me some inventions he was working on. He trusted me and he wanted me to see these things. He was a brilliant guy and he was trying to help me.

I thought wow, my ship has finally come in. I got a call from the writer who was going to do the business plan. We were going through writing all the different parts of the plan and I was trying to get him to capture my vision.

Next I got a call from an artist to draw the pictures of the stage and other features. It was just before September semester started and he was moving to Toronto, taking college and university courses. I was a little concerned. He came down to my house to meet me. Mark hired him. Mark said to me "Don't worry about it just get the idea out. I'll handle the money."

He was also paying the writer. I don't know what arrangement had been made. The young artist said he could have something done in two weeks.

"This is what I want to do. How soon can you have something?" He said, "Two weeks." I said "Can you handle this and go to school?" He said, "I'll have something for you in two weeks."

While the writing and preliminary sketches were being done, Mark asked me to put some prices together to build a recording studio.

I'd started laying out my plans which also included having my own record label.

I want to buy a house and the $100,000 that he said originally he would invest went to $500,000 within a week and then it shot up to about $1,000,000 and then we were talking $4 million.

I could see this would set me up for life - a studio, a recording facility, a record label, my own publishing, a bus to travel in and everything altered and adjusted especially for me,

Anything that I needed was going to get taken care of, such as all the health issues, hiring someone to travel with me on the road.

Mark said the plan was getting bigger than he could handle and he suggested we need to find a big investor. I phoned a guy in Toronto who's an expert studio builder. He does all the wiring in the big studios, all the mechanics. I said I would hire him to help me do a quote for the business plan. He agreed to come and meet me. While I waited for him, the telephone rang and this guy said he hadn't left his home. I said, "Why not?"

He said, "You know what? I ain't coming."

I said, "Why?"

He said, "I think a war's breaking out. You'd better turn on your TV. I gotta go pick up my kids at school."

He seemed to be in a panic, like it was the end of the world. I turned on the TV and that was September 11th of course, and I don't have to explain what I saw. The second tower had just been hit and I watched the towers come down.

I turned the TV off and I thought about it for a minute. I thought well, the

# Shawn Brush

The models for the medicine show were very well done.

world's not gonna stop. I gotta see this through. I've got things happening.

Mark approved a deal with someone to build a model of the stage and studio. The project would take a while.

When we had originally met, Mark had said he was retiring from his position in his business and he was waiting on a lot of funds to be transferred into his account. He was going to put $400,000 of his own money into this plan. We were going to seek the investment from one big investor so the presentation plan had to be the best it could be for a one-time meeting with the big investor.

We'd do the presentation, show the model, tell the story and the whole Krooked Cowboy stage scene. The way it turned out was ironic. It was to be an old west medicine show and there was a wagon like an old medicine wagon.

In the old days people would sell snake oil. To attract a crowd a musician would play. The people would come up and the guy would do the sales pitch to sell the snake oil. I dreamed up a stage where everything would be working together. The stage would have the wagon on it where I would sit and sing. I was the musician to attract the crowd.

On the side of the stage there'd be a set of stairs that would be *The Wooden Hill*.

There was a train at the back of the stage that would work just like the *Train of Thought* and a whisky bar for singing the Tim Gibbons song.

There was the saloon for the background and the town. I had some dialogue and ideas for actors in between the songs. It was more of a Showboat idea. If I was going to go out and sell this show on the road, it would be a big event. It's

# The Krooked Cowboy

a show that people would want to come and see.

I could go out there and make a lot of money, but I didn't know how long I could go out and do that for. I wanted to make it a really special event, an entire story. The whole show would revolve around the Krooked Cowboy and the Krooked Cowboy is me. I'd sit on the stage playing the music.

The way I had it planned, it started out in the desert in the badlands in a campground, on the farmland. The Krooked Cowboy would be playing his songs by the campfire. The medicine wagon would pull up and the snake oil salesman would say, "Gee you play pretty good, you should help me sell my snake oil. You could play your music and you could get famous and go out in the world. You could help a lot of people and help me sell this snake oil."

The show was done in two parts, that's the first scene. I'd play my songs, just me and my guitar solo around the campfire. The snake oil salesman would say "Come on. I'm going to town and we're going to sell the snake oil." There'd be an intermission and the campfire would change into a town.

The second part of the show would start and I'd have the band play with me because the band would meet up with the snake oil salesman in town. I was the new singer to front the band and sell the snake oil. People would gather around and the way we had the stage set up, the audience was the crowd. In between the songs, the snake oil salesman would come out and try and sell them on this snake oil. Of course, there's a reason it's called snake oil. You know, it doesn't work, it's just alcohol. Anyway, for the remainder of the show, this snake oil salesman comes off as a fraud. The real thing that people are buying is the Krooked Cowboy and his music. Then the snake oil salesman is gone and I get the wagon and the snake oil and away I go to the next town.

It was planned that the studio would be our headquarters.

That September I had booked the Studio Theatre at Hamilton Place. It was my first big show in that kind of venue.

Earlier in the summer, Global TV got interested in The Krooked Cowboy project. They were looking for an original, inspirational story, and mine seemed to fit the bill. News reporter Gus Kim called me one day and said he had been talking to a friend of mine, Michael Shotten, who had told him about The Krooked Cowboy. Gus said he was looking at doing a 20-minute story about me. I was delighted. They came to the house to do interviews and shoot film. It was scheduled to run, but then 9/11 hit and it changed things. As the months passed by it kept getting smaller as Global tried to work it into their newscast.

# Shawn Brush

It went from 20 minutes, to 15, then to 10 and then five.

About two days before Christmas, Gus Kim called and said, 'We're going to air the story on December 23rd.' They finally ran it at two minutes and 30 seconds. It was a nice piece. And anyone who knows TV news will tell you that not many stories get two-and-a-half minutes devoted to them. I was happy.

It went on Global Ontario News, but certain affiliates picked it up. It really did give me some good exposure; I got emails from people in Vancouver and Montreal saying 'we saw you on TV.' There were comments like, 'our son has Morquio's Disease' . . . 'When are you coming to Vancouver?' The TV reporter Gus Kim called me and said, 'Winnipeg really liked the story. When are you coming? When are you going to do this tour?' They said, 'When you come, we'll promote the hell out of it.' I was excited. All these things were happening.

So the New Year started and this guy with the model was way behind. The director guy I met with back in September, had set a date for January 12th. We were going to do a video for the presentation, and Mark was still paying for all this.

We brought in a guy from Montreal who makes native dream catchers just to lend that added touch of authenticity to the video.

Mark hired a guy named Dave Ferri who owns Orchard Studios at Norval up near Georgetown to do the recording and shoot videos and do production work. Mark had also purchased an Indian headdress. He also bought a big funhouse mirror, the kind that show you thin and fat and then tall and short and that was going to be part of the lobby set up, where it would be like a carnival in the old west.

Mark was wheeling and dealing his bikes. He had a motorcycle for sale and was buying another one. He bought an ultra-light and he sold something else. All these things were going on.

We shot the video at night because I am more a night person.

The lady who had taken photographs at the concert was going to come up and do pictures behind the scenes – the Making of the Video. Mark got excited and hired a second cameraman to film the making of the video. We had three things going on at once.

Around October, I had put in my CD, *Shawn Brush Kutz*, for a Juno nomination.

# The Krooked Cowboy

Come January, we were doing this video shoot and I got a letter in the mail that said I made the first set of people that were being considered for nomination for a Juno. Everything was just on a positive note, couldn't be better.

I had a girl.

I was driving a Cadillac.

I had this business guy having all these things going on. I had the story on the news. Everything was just in fast forward. The future was looking bright. I was getting nervous, anxious and excited. Just the realm of emotions from one year to the next was the total reverse.

From the lowest of the lows to the highest of the highs.

A friend of mine got her beginner's license and I let her drive because the driving was getting to me and if I didn't have to drive it was all the better because I had more energy to handle the business. On certain days her kids would be with us and we'd go out to breakfast. I was like an instant family man.

I was living the millionaire dream. It was all going to happen. There were all these promises. Then Mark said he was having some marital problems and he was talking about moving and getting a divorce. He also started having problems with his eyes and he couldn't see. He went to the doctor and they were talking about doing surgery and he might go blind in one eye. He had suffered a blow to his head, or something, and he'd detached the retina and they were hoping it would re-attach. He was having his own problems.

The end of February came around and I was broke and Mark hadn't retired. He was having problems with his eye. He assured me that it was just a delay. It would only be a few days and he was waiting to get his money. He said, "I'm going to loan you $10,000 to keep you going." I said, "Ok!" A couple of weeks went by, it was March. The March Break came and my friend and her kids came and stayed at my house for 10 days.

Mark picked up  a bad cold and was sick and the money still hadn't come through. The other thing he had got me doing was he said, "How d'you feel about this girl? He talked to her, telling her it seemed like a match made in heaven. I started looking at houses.

We found some really nice places. We told Mark, "We've found a couple of places that would just be perfect. We want you to come out and look at them."

# Shawn Brush

The plan was Mark would move in with us and then after he got his divorce settled, he would move out and we would have the house. That was part of the deal. It was an extravagant gift and this was how Mark was talking.

When something sounds too good to be true, it usually is. The model guy still didn't have this model done. Mark said, "I haven't got the money yet. I've officially retired but we can't do anything until the model is done." I phoned the guy, bugging him to get the model done. He said, "I'm going as fast as I can." He's working away at the model. I get a phone call one day from this guy in Milton who had done the banners for me for my concert back in September. He was doing his income tax for the year and he said he never got paid for the banners. I said, "What?" He said, "Yes, I've got an outstanding bill here for a couple hundred bucks for the banners." I said, "Oh! I'll look into it." He said, "I've been phoning that Mark guy, I can't get hold of him." I said, "Oh, he's been busy, he's having some problems."

I phoned Mark and I said, "Yeah! Did you pay for that bill for the banners?" He said, "I forgot all about it. I'll take care of it." I didn't think about it. He said he'd take care of it. He was taking care of a lot of things.

I was holding my own and right now I was playing the waiting game. Everything started to get more delayed. The model wasn't getting done. Mark wasn't getting his money. He was having more problems with his eye and with his personal life.

We arranged for Mark to come and look at a house we thought would be appropriate. He didn't show up and we're standing there with the real estate agent waiting.

I phoned him. He was sick in bed. He had the flu. He couldn't make it. I was starting to get agitated. I'd spent the last six months sitting and waiting. I'd done all the work. I'd got things done and I was waiting on people. Things were out of my control. I was broke. My mom and dad were good to me.

Mark kept saying he was going to lend me this $10,000. I said to Mark, "You know $10,000 won't even cover the debts I owe people." The amount of money, personal loans from friends and family, you know $3,000 to fix my car so $10,000 was nothing. He said, "You know, I'm going to have some money at the end of March." The end of March rolled around and he said, "Well we can't do anything until we get that model." I said, "Well, have you got that money?" He said, "No, I don't have it yet." Then this guy phoned me again about the banners. "Yeah, he never came, he never phoned me, I can't get a hold of Mark." So I phoned Mark. I said, "The guy from the banners called again." He said "Oh, yeah, I gotta take care of that. I'll go over and talk to him." It would take another couple of months before he paid this guy off, the couple hundred bucks from back in September.

The other thing that happened was that the model was finally ready. The model guy phoned me up and told me it was going to be $3,500 for the model. I phoned Mark and I said "the model's ready. Do you want me to go pick it up?" He said, "No, no I want to bring it here to my house. I got a special place for it. I got a place all set aside."

Then the model guy phoned me again and he said, "Mark still hasn't come to get the model." This guy worked really hard on the model. He spent a lot of time on it, a lot of detail. It had taken four months to make.

I phoned Mark again and I said, "Is this going to be a problem?" He said, "No, No, I'll take care of it. I'll go visit him."

I phoned the guy and he said, "Yes, Mark gave me a cheque." I wasn't going to wait. I phoned my friend Bert, he had a pick-up truck and my friend Tom Pet. We went to pick it up near Acton and we got the model in the truck and everything looked great. It was in a big box with carrying handles like a crate and we needed a truck to pick it up. We drove back and Tom helped unload it. I opened it and set the model up and I showed Bert and Tom. They knew I'd been working hard for months on this big project and they saw the model and they said, "Is that ever cool!"

I told them the whole concept. They were impressed. Then I packed it all up and put it away. At the same time I should have been feeling good, but all these promises weren't coming to fruition.

The next day sure enough, the model guy phoned me and said, "The cheque bounced." I phoned Mark and said, "The cheque bounced." He said "Oh, I must have taken it from the wrong account. I should have paid from the other account." That took a couple of weeks but finally the guy got paid.

The video, we finally got that done but there had been all kinds of delays.

Talk about stress. My mood was changing and I was starting to get a little bitter and agitated because nothing was happening and I was just sitting and waiting and the worst thing you can do is to make Shawn Brush wait, after everything I'd been through. Things were starting to fall apart.

The demise of the $4,000,000 promise.

When you want something in the worst way, it's usually how you get it.

Hamilton Music Award winner in 2008, Lori Yates, with Shawn

# 22

# Hurry up - and wait!

I have been in a couple of movies. The first was an extra in a crowd scene when they were shooting *The Air Up There* starring Kevin Bacon at the Copps Coliseum in Hamilton.

I went down and sat in the crowds and got paid $80 and a free lunch.

It was okay, nothing special. Lots of hanging around. Movie making is painfully slow.

The other was a bit role in a movie shot in Toronto.

An agent who was working out of an office in Burlington asked me to be an extra in another movie, but I said I wasn't interested. She kept asking me, but I said I am doing my music thing, and I wasn't interested in a movie, unless it pays well.

I am a unique guy. I am a little person, I am a specialty. That's what she had been telling me so if she could get me something that required someone like me then it would have to pay well.

I said I was not driving to Toronto for $50 or $100.

She said she would call me if anything came up. I figured I had heard the last from her.

However, a couple of weeks later she called about a Dan Ackroyd movie being

167

filmed and asked me if I was interested.

I said I would do it provided it met my criteria: it has to pay well . . . you have to give me lots of lead-time…you can't call me on Tuesday night and ask me to be there on Wednesday.

She phoned me and said in about 10 days or two weeks they are going to be doing the movie with Dan Ackroyd.

She said they wanted me to play a waiter in a Speak Easy in the 1920s.

That sounded good.

I didn't phone them, I figured they would call me.

They did.

The wardrobe lady called and said, "I need to know your measurements."

"What for?"

"Aren't you coming in to do the movie tomorrow?"

"I don't know anything about it, my agent hasn't phoned me."

"Well, your name is on the list and they are counting on you being there tomorrow."

"What time am I supposed to be there?"

"Two o'clock is the casting call."

"Where is it?"

"Down on Cherry Street in Toronto."

I told her my sizes and, of course, they don't have anything that would fit me.

I said I would bring some clothes with me.

She says, "It is a 1920s speak easy, if you have a black suit and shoes."

I said I would bring a whole bunch of clothes.

So here I am a specialty getting all the info second hand and bringing my whole wardrobe.

I said I would be there and I am a man of my word.

I will never forget this. I can tell you the date, it was August 16 and it was the Friday because the CNE started the next day.

# The Krooked Cowboy

I went and played music Thursday night, and I was dog-tired, but I went to bed and got up around noon. I had something to eat, put my suit in the car, as well as a black jacket and a couple of dress shirts, a pair of black boots I had made in Toronto when I was 17, a pair of black leather Beatle boots, and I jumped in the car.

I drove to Cherry Street down by the docks and they told me where to park. They told me the name of the guy to look for and said the movie was the *Man In The Attic*.

I come onto the movie lot and I recognize the building in Toronto's Distillery District. I have seen it in all kinds of movies. It gets used quite a bit in big budget movies.

I went onto the lot and said I was looking for so-and-so the casting guy. He is over on the east end of the lot, down at the back.

So I walked all the way down to the other end of the lot and someone said he was over the other end of the lot. That's where wardrobe is.

I walk all the way back and I am not in a good mood. I get in there and I ask for him and he is on the couch, talking on the phone, "You must be Shawn. We don't need you until 6 o'clock so you may as well relax."

I went to sleep in my car. I was pooped. I lay down and put my feet up. Put the windows down. I had my suit on the garment hook so there was some shade.

I fell asleep for an hour or two.

I got up at around 3:30 and I was hungry. I looked around and it was pretty quiet.

I went to get something to eat. I drove over to Church Street and grabbed a bowl of rice and some chicken. Then I walked up Church Street into the pawnshops near Queen Street.

Then it was 4:30 so I thought I would drive back.

I get back to the movie lot and a girl comes running up, "I've been looking all over for you. I'll help you with your clothes. We'll carry them all in."

She tells me that I have a nice jacket. "Put that shirt on. These are the boots."

The casting guy came in and he was red, you could see he had been upset, and he said, "We were looking all over for you. You can't leave a movie set."

"I told you I was going to sleep in my car and you told me you didn't need me

169

till 6 o'clock. Here I am now let's get it done."

So it's six o'clock and they've got this movie set. They have been set up since 6 a.m.

Then I find out this isn't the Dan Ackroyd movie, this is going to be an HBO movie called *Man In The Attic* with Neil Patrick Harris (Doogie Howser} and he was the big man in the movie.

It was a love story about a woman who kept the guy locked in the attic for 20 years and had an affair with him. Neil Patrick Harris was the *Man In The Attic*.

They were now moving inside the building to shoot the speak easy scene, like Chicago in the 1930s.

They wanted me in the film because the Mafia would hire a little guy and take care of him. They would look out for him and give him a job.

I was going to be a waiter. Everyone was sitting down and I would be walking around in the background.

The way they did it was very bizarre. It was interesting to watch how the movie was made. They had four or five main characters around a table and they would shoot the dialogue of one person and they had one camera set up to film the person talking.

Then they would turn the table and change the background, so they would move the extras out and take the bar and move it from one end of the room to the other end of the room. Then they would film the next person at the table. They would move everything again and film the third, and do the same for the fourth person.

It was really a lot of work.

It started at 6 p.m. and they were running a bit late, so I put on my black suit, my black boots and my white shirt and they told me where to walk, take an order and deliver a drink. They gave me a tray.

"Action!"

They had hundreds of extras. It was a big warehouse set up as a bar supposedly underground in a cavern.

So I walked onto the set and because it was all concrete floors and wooden pallets my heels on my boots were making a noise.

The director yells, "Cut! Wardrobe. Get some foam on his shoes."

# The Krooked Cowboy

They were putting on this foam with glue - onto my own shoes!

They said don't worry it will come off.

I had had these shoes handmade when I was 17. My dad had taken me to Toronto because I have a very wide, but short foot.

To get shoes made I had dressy shoes for the first time in my life and these were the boots I was wearing to do this movie thing – and they are putting foam on them!

I had a pair of snakeskin cowboy boots made as well. At the same place on Wellesley Street called Elvis' Shoes.

When the foam was on the shoes they said they were not going to use me right away. "Hang tight, we'll get to you."

When it got to 8 o'clock I was getting bored watching this movie stuff and I went outside with the lighting guys.

They told me the reality of the movie business was 'hurry up and wait.'

It was exactly the kind of day I was having.

Somebody came up and said they were going to break for supper.

They had hundreds of people there and they called Swiss Chalet and got 200 quarter chicken dinners and 200 submarines from Mr. Submarine.

About a half-hour later the dinner arrived and they took a break.

The foam was wearing off my shoes.

About 9:30 they started filming again.

At 11 someone came running out and said they are going to use me.

I go in and I do the walk through and they said, "Wardrobe. We need more foam on the shoes."

I was thinking I could be playing music at the Ragin' Cajun right now.

This is what I am doing on a Friday night? I'd better be getting paid well.

They said we want you to walk by the main table and walk over here take the drink off the tray and put it here. They use apple juice for beer.

"Action!"

I put the drink down.

"Cut."

# Shawn Brush

Now we want you to walk this way and put the drink on the table and take an order. Don't say anything. Just take an order. It was silent. They would add the voices and background noise later.

Just the main characters were talking, and that's why I needed the foam on my boots so I wouldn't get on the sound track.

"Action!"

I walk through ... I put the drink down and pretend to take an order. I walk off screen.

"Cut. That was great."

Now walk back through and put the drink on the table that you took the order from and walk out the other side.

"Action!"

I walk through, put the drink down and it was a real success.

They are just finishing up this last scene. It is about 11:30 and they were finishing for the day.

The director gets up from his chair and comes right over to me and says, "We couldn't have done it without you. That was great."

So he was really enthusiastic. He really liked it.

Thanks, where do I get paid?

I found the casting guy and everyone goes in there and gets paid in cash.

He said we couldn't pay you here because you are a specialty, we have to send it in and we will then send you a cheque.

Now I have to wait.

"Oh, by the way, I left a lot of really nasty messages when we couldn't find you this afternoon. Disregard them."

I get home and it is after midnight.

It is my mom and dad's phone line.

Here's the guy on the phone. Calling me a four-letter word and telling me in no uncertain terms that I was not going to work in the industry again.

It was just bizarre. He phoned the agency that was supposed to be looking after me and, of course, she phoned and was cursing and swearing at me.

172

# The Krooked Cowboy

This whole thing turned me off.

It took me three weeks to get all the foam off my shoes.

Then they phoned me and asked me to go in and do a commercial.

"No."

"It's a really good thing. They want you to play a mini Elvis. It's a music thing you can play your guitar."

"No, I am not interested."

Even my mom said I should go.

I said, "No. I am not going."

I am waiting for my cheque.

I still don't have the cheque. But the agent kept phoning me and offering me jobs.

It had been three weeks and I phoned ACTRA and they had my cheque. But they said they didn't have my SIN number, my agent had not given them the information.

I gave them my SIN number over the phone and they mailed my cheque. It was for $100.

I didn't think that was right. I phoned the agent and I said I thought I was a specialty. I brought my own wardrobe; it has taken me a month to get the foam off my shoes.

She says, "You still owe me 10 per cent."

She wanted her 10 lousy dollars.

I gave her $10 and said don't call me any more.

They kept phoning.

They wanted me to do the Elvis commercials, then they were doing a Christmas movie and they wanted me to be an elf.

The wardrobe people were phoning me. They said it was going to pay 10 grand and you only have to work 10 days.

After the experience I had been through I told them to leave me alone.

# Shawn Brush

SHORN SHAWN !!! Shawn decided
to go for the Brush cut one day
after a lifetime of long hair. He liked
the new look so much that he even
named his CD Brush Kutz.

## 23

# Parking problems

Next time you park in a handicap parking spot, think about me - and others like me - who really need these special spaces.

I am not looking for any sympathy, but while it might not hurt you to walk 40 or 50 yards longer, it takes a lot out of me.

And when I park in a regular spot, my handicap permit doesn't count for anything. I can't reach the parking meter money slots in the lots where there are no attendants.

I can't tell you how many parking tickets I have had, even when I park in a handicapped spot.

The last time was in the summer of 2003 – and it was a big one. Three-hundred dollars for parking in a handicapped zone at Costco. This was particularly disturbing because the store management would not do anything about it. I went to the provincial police, who sent me to the city police.

What had happened is that my licence had slipped down, because I was in a new car and I had not secured it properly. The person who wrote the ticket claimed he couldn't see the expiry date – even though he admitted seeing the handicapped permit.

# Shawn Brush

It's one of those things that appear to be a no-brainer. When they see me come into the police station, there should be no mistaking that I am the rightful owner of the handicapped permit. Oh, I don't doubt that some people misuse these permits. And, of course, many people park in handicapped spaces illegally.

But when it is so obvious that I am not trying to scam the authorities, surely they would give me a break.

I find that I don't get many breaks in my hometown of Burlington. But other neighbouring communities treat me better.

There was one time in Welland where the person in the traffic office took one look at me and ripped up the ticket.

When I told this story to the person I was talking to about the Costco ticket, he said, "You know you could go to jail for ripping up that ticket."

I cancelled my membership at Costco when they didn't offer any help. It made me feel good to do that. However, when I look back I think of what a few kind words at the right time may have done to change the tone of the entire situation.

On another occasion I got a parking ticket for parking in a public parking lot in downtown Burlington.

It was 2000 and I was still trying to get out and play. I got a call one night, from a blues singer who needed a guitar player. She asked if I could come and play for the night. This was about 8 o'clock at night. She was playing at a bistro down at Brant Street and Lakeshore Road. It was one of those places that would never hire me for some reason.

Right on the corner of Lakeshore and Brant there used to be a gas station. It's closed up. It was a privately owned public parking lot where you bought a ticket from the machine and put it on your windshield.

I parked my car and the funny thing was, there was a big sign that read 'Public Parking, get your ticket from the machine.' So that's what I did – or planned to do. There was no handicapped parking. I managed to get as close as I could to the building because I had to carry my guitar in something like a backpack.

I went up to get a ticket from the machine but I couldn't reach the machine to put in my money. So I left my handicapped-parking permit on the dash and I went in and played the gig. When I came out, I had a parking ticket for thirty or forty bucks. I said 'I'm not paying that, I'm going to fight that.'

I went down to City Hall in Burlington. Everywhere else I'd ever been there was never a problem. They'd just rip up the ticket right there, just dismiss it. I went in and there was a guy there. I told him I could not reach the parking meters to put in any money. They were too high

He said, "Well, you're going to have to go to court and fight that."

I said "What?"

He said, "Yes, you'll have to fight that."

I said, "There's no handicapped parking in there and a handicapped individual can't reach the meter to pay and it's a public parking lot."

He said, "I know it's a public parking lot. But it's privately owned. You'll have to take it up with the owner."

I said, "This is stupid."

He gave me the name of the company that owned the parking lot.

I was pretty perturbed by this. I'd never had a problem anywhere else with parking tickets, Toronto, Welland, Hamilton, anywhere else, except my hometown of Burlington.

I phoned the guy who owned the lot. He said, "There's nothing I can do about it. I authorized the city to ticket anyone who parks there illegally. I don't get any money from that. That goes to the city."

I go back to City Hall and I talk to the guy and I say, "Who gets the money?" He says, "So much goes to the province, so much goes to the city."

I said, "So, you're actually making a profit off me and I haven't broken any laws. I needed to park there."

He said, "Well, there's nothing I can do. I can't rip that ticket up. I'd go to jail." I said, "Well, can I talk to the guy who wrote the ticket." I told him that I got a ticket one time and the police officer said, "Go and talk to the guy who wrote the ticket." The police station is right around the corner from City Hall, I went over there to see the bylaw officer who'd written the ticket.

I said to the guy, "I parked my car here on such and such a day. I got this ticket."

"What? You didn't pay?"

"Yeah, well, I couldn't reach the machine."

"Why didn't you get someone else to pay for you?"

# Shawn Brush

"Well, it was late at night. There was no one else around and I'm an independent kind of person. There's handicapped spots in there that haven't been marked and the guy told the city not to ticket anyone with handicapped permits."

"Oh I don't know anything about that. I was never told anything like that."

"Well, is there anything you can do?"

"Oh no, I can't change the ticket, I could go to jail for something like that."

"Well, what's a guy supposed to do? I had to go on into that restaurant that night and I'm a disabled guy and I parked there and I can't reach the machine, even in a wheelchair. Nobody can pay in a wheelchair and it's a public parking lot."

"Well, you park somewhere else then. There's a lot two blocks down the street where you can park."

I tried to explain to him that I can't walk two blocks, but he wasn't listening. We had a few words. I wasn't very happy.

So I went back to City Hall and I talked to this same guy who said he couldn't rip the ticket up and that it wasn't really the city's problem.

I had talked to the owner of the lot.

I had talked to the bylaw officer.

They were all refusing to budge. They were convinced that if they ripped up the parking ticket they would go to jail. I wondered who was running city hall in Burlington. I thought it must be a pretty miserable place to work if everyone seemed scared to make a decision for fear of being thrown in jail.

I stated my case again. This time I was getting louder and started getting pretty obnoxious at what to me was absolute disdain for a taxpayer trying to make a point.

Then he said, "You know what? You know what I'm going to do?"

I said, "What?"

He said, "I'm going to rip this ticket up for good public relations. Just to make you happy."

I said, "Good!"

So he ripped up the ticket and I said, "And you didn't have the authority to do that before - or you could go to jail?"

# The Krooked Cowboy

The mentality of parking ticket people. I thought to myself, what a little customer service training could do for Burlington's image.

Don't get me wrong. I am all for big fines for people who park illegally – and particularly for people who park in handicapped areas. I was really pleased to see the City of Toronto triple its fines for parking in handicapped spots in March 2008. I think a first time offence is now $450. But will it stop people taking those special spots? I doubt it. Some folks just don't care – or don't realize how critical those spots are for the people with disabilities.

I just hope that those handing out tickets are given some kind of training to recognize when a person who is obviously handicapped, or physically challenged is given a ticket by mistake.

I don't want to create a holier than thou impression of me, particularly on this parking problem.

I understand as well as anyone, I guess, the importance for the handicapped spots to be reserved for those who need them.

But I am like every other driver when it comes to finding a place to park – and I am always looking to park as close to where I am going as possible.

A few years ago I went to Toronto to see an agent. She had an agency called Star Tracks and it was just for disabled actors and actresses. She knew some people in the music business and she was disabled herself. She was a little person.

She got work for people with disabilities in commercials. Her whole agency was based in this unique specialty, handicapped people, little people, deaf people, blind people and she was interested in maybe helping someone in the music business.

I had read about her in one of the Toronto newspapers so I went down to visit her. She lived near Front Street in an apartment building right beside a TV studio where they used to tape the Dini Petti Show.

When I arrived there was no parking for about three blocks. I wouldn't be able to walk three blocks in Toronto, then or now. It would take me an hour.

Right outside her place there are big sidewalks that must be 30 or 40 feet wide in some spots. I saw several lighting trucks from a production crew were pulled up on the sidewalk.

I was driving a big Pontiac Parisienne. I drove right up on the sidewalk. Pulled right up in front of where they were shooting the movie. They had all kinds of police standing around.

Before I got out of my car I noticed my briefcase was on the front seat and it was full of all kinds of letters from publishing companies. I threw them up on the dashboard. There was a lot of official paper work from Warner Bros and others.

I walked up to a couple of lighting guys and said, "How are things going?"

They said, "Oh pretty good."

I asked, "They started in there without me?"

They replied, "Oh, we don't know man, we're just doing lighting."

I said, "Ok, well, is it all right if I borrow some pylons from you?"

They said "Sure." They handed me some orange pylons with Toronto Film Company on them. I walked over to my car and I put the pylons all around my car.

A police officer was watching me. He was about to walk over there and tell me I couldn't park there, but he saw me put the pylons around my car.

They were shooting the movie right beside the building I had to go into. Everybody watched me park there. Nobody knew who I was. I walked over to the building where they were shooting the movie and I said, "Do they need me in there yet?" I gave him a name and he said, "I'll just go and check." I said "Ok! I'm just going to go into this building next door, there's somebody over here I've got to meet." They said "Oh Ok!" They ran away with a clipboard and a magic marker.

I waved at the cop and he must have said to himself, 'Okay, he must be part of the film.'

I went in and had my meeting with the manager and she said, "Are you interested in the movies?" I said, "No I'm not interested, I just want to do the music." She took some information off me. She never really did anything for me. She tried to do some stuff. She knew some people in the music industry, but it never came to fruition.

I came out of the meeting and everybody looked at me. I picked up the pylons, I opened the trunk of my car and I threw the pylons into my car. I yelled out of the window, "Tell them I'll be back later" and I drove away.

I kept those pylons for years and any time I ever went to Toronto, I never worried about parking. I just parked wherever I wanted and I put the film cones out and never got tickets. I don't know what happened to them. I lost them, they got wrecked or something. Somebody might have stolen them from me.

So, you see, I have sympathy with everyone trying to park a car . . . but I ask just to have a thought for me – and all people like me who don't have regular mobility – when you go to park in a handicapped spot.

Shawn likes visiting Niagara Falls . . . but this, in reality, would be too close!

# Shawn's hoping for a Brush with fame

• • • • •

Shawn Brush

local
BEAT

Local media, especially the Hamilton Spectator and the Burlington Post, have been very complimentary to Shawn over the years.

DAVID COCHRANE

Burlington Post
Backbeat
Sept. 4, '98

# Seeking a Brush with success

H

## Every song a gem on Shawn Brush album

### The Wooden Hill

The Wooden Hill
Shawn Brush

### New folk fest to benefit Artery

## Singer hopes for brush with fame

By DENNIS SMITH
Burlington Post writer

Shawn Brush enjoys playing all kinds of music, and it seems all kinds of people enjoy hearing him.

His mix of bluegrass, country, folk and rock may not be hit chart material. But Brush has received fan mail from such unlikely places as Tacoma, Wash., West Virginia, Ohio, and even France. He finds the letters very gratifying.

"You're riding tall in the saddle my friend," wrote one admirer after a recent Brush show in Hamilton.

"I'm not mainstream and I'm more of a songwriter," said Brush. "A songwriter's life is 99 per cent rejection, but a few bluegrass bands have played my songs."

In fact, Brush has won a couple of Central Canada Bluegrass Awards for his tunes, and has had several other nominations.

The 26-year-old has been playing guitar nearly half his life — he was taught how to play by a cab driver named Dan. When growing up, the former Assumption and M.M. Robinson high school student took a taxi to school every day.

### Plays many styles

"The guitar has always been there," he said. "One night I'll hang out with some rock and roll guys, and another night I'll do bluegrass."

Brush also was pedal steel guitar player for the country band Timberline.

But he works solo and limits his gigs ... his condition makes hauling ... ling too much

## Shawn's big voice can make you hurt

Paul Wilson

# Shawn Brush

Shawn with his best friend growing up, Gary Tarnawski. Notice the difference in Shawn's stature with his peer. You can also see the ox-legged stance which surgeries helped to correct.

# 24

# Morquio - a medical appendix

Morquio syndrome (mucopolysaccharidosis type IV; MPS IV) is an inherited disease of metabolism in which the body is missing - or doesn't have enough of - a substance needed to break down long chains of sugar molecules called glycoaminoglycans.

It is an autosomal recessive trait, which means both parents must pass on the defective gene in order for the disease to establish.

It is a rare form of dwarfism that was first described, simultaneously and independently, in 1929, by Luis Morquio in Montevideo, Uraguay, and by James Frederick Brailsford in Birmingham, England. They both recognized the occurrence of corneal clouding, aortic valve disease, and urinary excretion of kerartan sulfate, in several patients.

Morquio causes severe growth retardation (adult height 82 to 115 cm) . . . the skull is unusually thick and dense . . . there is clouding of the eyes . . . hearing loss . . . the liver is slightly enlarged . . . multiple abnormalities of the spine . . . the chest is pigeon shaped . . . prominent lower face . . . abnormally short neck . . . flat feet . . . weakness of the legs and abnormal development of the growing ends of the long bones.

There is no specific treatment for Morquio syndrome, symptoms are treated as they occur. It occurs in 1 in 250,000 births.

# Shawn Brush

Morquio patients appear healthy at birth, but children are evaluated by the second or third year of life when spinal deformity begins to be noticeable.

Following are excerpts from numerous hospital visits I made over the years. I thought this might give you an idea of the care I have received. It gets a little technical, but generally these reports are written so the patient and parents can understand.

**Hospital for Sick Children, Toronto:**

**Admitted 12 April 1972**

**Discharged 2 May 1972**

Final Diagnosis: Spondyloepiphyseal dysplasia

This 2 ½ year old boy was admitted for investigation of a rare and insofar undiagnosed bone deformity.

There was a normal birth history and no evidence of consanguinity of the parents. His milestones had been fairly normal, except for delay of speech development.

In August 1971, almost at two years of age, the parents and other relatives noticed a waddling abnormality of gait with almost a sitting posture, when walking, and also bow legs. Also a lumbar lordosis was noted, and prominent bony protuberances at ankles, knees and wrists.

X-rays revealed abnormal findings and a type of osteochondral dystrophy, and he was referred here for complete metabolic work-up, with the possibility of Morquio's disease.

On examination, a robust looking, 2 ½ year-old boy in no distress. No pallor, cysnosis or jaundice. His weight was on the 25th percentile and height less than the third percentile. Blood pressure 110/65/ Pulse 110 and regular.

Examination of head and neck revealed a chubby face, symmetrical. Pupils were equal and reactive. Eye movements were normal. The fundi were normal and there were no cataracts. Ears were normal. The tonsils were enlarged. But not infected. The chest was clear. Heart sounds were normal. The femorals were palpable. The abdomen was soft, non-tender. Mo hepatosplenomegaly.

186

# The Krooked Cowboy

Bowel sounds were normal. Genitalia were those of a normal male.

Neurological: He was mentally o.k. and appeared bright. The rest of the neurological examination was within normal limits. The deep tendon reflexes were symmetrical.

Skeletal system showed that he had a short neck and evidence of light scoliosis. The upper extremities appeared normal, except for widening and thickening of the distal ulna and radius. The hip movements were normal. There was no click. There was slight bowing of the femura. He walked with knee flexion and there was a definite knee click with full extension. Also, there was thickening of both malleoli. There was a full range of movement of all the joints.

Lab investigations: Hemoglobin 12.8/ Sed rate 21. WBC 10.9, Differential was normal and platelets were normal. Fasting blood sugar was 88, 86 and 144 mg on different occasions. T3 and T4 were normal. Electrolytes were normal. Vision was 20. Urine pH was 9, and repeated urine pH was 8. Serum creatine was 0.6, calcium 108, phosphorus 5.1, magnesium 1.7, Serum protein electrophoresis was normal. 24-hour urine collection for mucopolysaccharides was abnormal on two occasions, being 11.7 and 11.1. This is considered to be 2 times or 3 times normal. However, on these two occasions the urine volume was greater than normal and therefore this result was not considered valid. 24-hour urine was repeated for mucopolysaccharides and at this time it was normal.

Eye consultation revealed no ocular findings, suggestive of mucopolysaccharidosis.

He was also seen by the Genetic Services, who are going to interview the parents also.

Other investigations included a urine culture which was negative. Throat swab was negative. Urine osmolatity was 744 milliosmols.

Psychological testing revealed average intellectual ability.

Skeletal survey and metabolic bone survey revealed that this is one variety of what has been called by Runin 'spondyloepiphyseal dysplasia.' This presents as a bizarre disorder of bone growth involving articular cartilage, epiphyses and growth plates.

There was an epiphyseal and metaphyseal growth disturbance. The bone texture was abnormal. The most striking metaphyseal abnormalities were in the hips and ankles and the most striking epiphyseal disturbances were in the multiple bodies.

The skull X-ray was normal.

At the end of all the tests it was felt that he basically has a bone disease and that there is no evidence of any metabolic disease. He was seen by Dr. Bobechko who will continue to follow him and see him again in one month's time in his clinic. Dr. Fraser will see him in one year's time and reassess him.

Final diagnosis: Spondyloepiphyseal dysplasia. To be followed up by Dr. Bobechko in one month's time, and the family doctor.

*S. Khan, M.D.*

**Hospital for Sick Children**

**Surgical out-patient clinic**

**8 October 1974**

This five-year-old boy has spondylo-epipyseal dysplasia. He is not getting into any major problems on the films that were sent with him today. He has a bit of scoliosis, but this is certainly under good control. His legs tend to have a genu valgum, but likewise this is not severe, and nothing need be done for the present. He will be followed along by Dr. MacIntyre.

*W.P. Bobechko, M.D., F.R.C.S.(C)*

**Hospital for Sick Children**

**Surgical out-patient clinic**

**1 November 1976**

This 7-year-old boy is seen in clinic for spondylo-epiphyseal dysplasia. Since his last visit one year ago, Shawn has been managing very well and has kept up with his peers in school.

# The Krooked Cowboy

On today's visit, Shawn is a short, seven-year-old boy. With very marked lumbar lordosis and a waddling type of gait. He walks with both knee and hip flexion contractures. Examination of his back shows that he has a scoliosis in the thoracolumbar region with a moderate degree of rib hump. The scoliosis measures 53 deg. He has really prominent lordosis. There is no evidence of any neurological deficit.

Examination of the hips shows that he has about 20 deg. hip flexion contracture, bilaterally. He has good flexion and extension, but has 0 deg. of abduction in both hips. He has limited internal and external rotation. Examination of the knees revealed a loss of 20 deg. of extension in both knees. He has a loud clank in his knee when the knees are extended. He has a marked degree of genu valgum involving both knees. Feet are normal.

X-rays shows he has a 52 deg., sharp right thoracolumbabar curve. There is no evidence of any spondylolisthesis. He has marked lumbar lordosis. The comparison of the x-rays with the previous ones show and increase of 3 deg. and a curvature of his scoliosis. Orthoroentgenoghrams show marked genu valgum bilaterally, with epiphseal dysplasia of the hips, distal femoral and proximal tibial epiphysis.

Dr. Bobechko spoke with Shawn's mother, and he told her that Shawn should be watched closely, particularly with regard to his scoliosis and his genu valgum. He was to have orthoroentgenograms of both lower extremities, and x-rays (3-foot standing), of the spine on his next visit.

*C. Rao, M.D.*

**Hospital for Sick Children**

**Surgical out-patient clinic**

**7 June 1977**

This 7 ½ year-old boy returns to the clinic today regarding assessment for his spondylo-epiphyseal dysplasia. A prime concern with this boy, in the past, has been his lumbar scoliosis and his genu valgus. The parents state today that he runs and plays quite energetically with other children, indulging in most normal activities. They feel that perhaps his lumbar lordosis is increasing and that his buttocks are becoming m ore prominent. They have not noticed a change in his knock-knee deformity.

On examination today he stands with rather marked lumbar lordosis and walks in a moderate crouch. He has hip flexion deformities in the range of 40-50 deg, bilaterally which accounts for his lordosis, Hip abduction bilaterally is about 15 deg. There is no rotation. Knees and feet are acceptable. The degree of genu valgum today is also acceptable.

His lumbar spine displays a left lumbar curve of 50 deg. This is unchanged from one year ago.

Dr. Bobechko told the parents that we would like to see him again in one year's time. At that time, consideration will be given to performing subtrochanteric femoral osteotomies. This would allow him to straighten up when he walks and obliterate much of his lumbar lordosis.

Return in one year. X-ray of legs and three-foot AP and lateral of the spine.

*J.K. Stapleton, M.D.*

**Hospital for Sick Children**

**Surgical out-patient clinic**

**27 June 1978**

Shawn is now 8 ½ years of age and has spondylo-epiphyseal dysplasia. His lumbar scoliosis has remained unchanged at about 50 degrees. Neurologically reflexes and gait is normal.

He does however have marked hip and knee flexion deformity with hips being 45 hip flexion deformity and knees about 30. There is limitation of abduction of both hips as well.

One wonders about the justifiability of doing extension osteotomies of both femora at the hip and knee levels to correct this and I suspect that it would not be justified because he gets along too well.

There is no question however that the scoliosis is going to progress at some stage and he will require Harrington instrumentation with or without fusion initially. I will see him back in nine months. Should have three-foot standing films of the spine, an orthoronentgenograsm and eventually clinical photographs.

*W.P. Bobechko, M.D.*

**Hospital for Sick Children**

**Admitted 6 September 1979**

**Discharged 29 September 1979**

History: The patient was a 10-year-old boy with known Morquio's syndrome who came to the emergency department after a fall off his bicycle. A fracture of his left femur was diagnosed in the emergency department and the Orthopedic Service was consulted.

On examination, the patient was noted to have a short stature. Head was normocephalic, no problem with cranial nerves. He had no obvious swelling of the left thigh with crepitus on moving the left femur.

The patient was placed in skin traction and was put in a body frame and was kept in a Trendelenburg position for the time until September 27th. During that time, x-ray of the fracture with alignment was checked. On September 27th it was felt that there was enough callous and the alignment was satisfactory. The patient was taken to the Fracture Room where the hip spica was applied and following this, the patient was sent home.

The patient will be followed by Dr. Bobechko in his clinic.

Final Diagnosis: Fracture left femur. His main problem is spondyloepiphyseal dysokasua,

Operation: None.

Treatment: Skin traction followed by Hip Spica Immobilization.

Complications: Nil.

*A. Tountas, M.D.*

# Shawn Brush

**Hospital for Sick Children**

**Surgical out-patient clinic**

**14 November 1979**

Shawn is 10 years old with Morquio's syndrome. He sustained a fracture of his left femur of September 6th. 1979. He was taken to Emergency Department and put into a Thomas splint traction and after three weeks he was put into a spica and was sent home in a spica. Today, the spica was removed. X-rays were taken which show nice callus, but not sound enough. The position looks nice in the a.p. and in the laterals, there is bayonet position with shortening of almost one inch.

Dr. Bobechko saw the patient and told the parents that from now on, he can start mobilization slowly and he should stay another week at home and then he can go back to school without taking any gym classes or any kind of sporting activity.

We will see him back in six months time and ortho leg x-rays will be taken on arrival. We will take a three-foot spine x-ray at the same time.

*D. Hendel, M.D.*

**Hospital for Sick Children**

**Surgical out-patient clinic**

**15 December 1980**

Shawn had the cast removed today from his right leg following a primal tibial osteotomy and this portion is nicely aligned. He is going to start weightbearing on it. He now requires second distal right tibial drill osteotomy and he will be admitted for this on January 4th.

Because of his short leg, he will probably require a long leg cast, but we may just get away with a below-knee for six weeks.

*W. Bobechko, M.D.*

# The Krooked Cowboy

**Hospital for Sick Children**

**Discharge Report**

**27 October 1980**

Admitting history:

This is an eleven-year-old boy with a spondyloepiphyseal dysplasia who was admitted for correction of a valgus deformity of his right knee.

His past health included a history of a fractured left femur.

Functional inquiry was otherwise unremarkable.

General physical examination showed him to be a dwarf young man in no distress. He had a short neck with a good range of motion. The remainder of his general physical examination was unremarkable.

Musculoskeletal examination showed several of the features of Morquio's syndrome with a broad, barrel-shaped short trunk, short limbs. He had a 5 degree flexion deformity of his right hip with 40 degrees of valgus in the right knee with a 20 degree flexion deformity and some moderate ligamentous laxity. There was a varus deformity of about 30-40 degrees in the right ankle with a long right fibula.

The child was taken to the operating room the day following his admission (22 October 1980) where a high tibial osteotomy and fibular osteotomy was carried out correcting the valgus deformity of his knee and also some of the flexion deformity.

He was immobilized in a long leg cast post operatively. When he was ambulated on crutches, he was discharged home. Our plan is to bring him back to clinic in six weeks time. His cast will be removed at that time. We will probably send him out for a period of mobilization and will return him to hospital shortly thereafter for a valgus osteotomy of his ankle.

Final diagnosis:

Spondyloepiphyseal dysplasia with valgus deformity of right knee.

Operative procedure:

Right tibial osteotomy.

*M.G. Martin, M.D.*

# Shawn Brush

**Hospital for Sick Children**

**Discharge Report**

**9 January 1981**


This 11 year-old boy has spondyloepiphyseal dysplasia. He was admitted to hospital (4 January 1981) for treatment of his right leg. A severe valgus deformity of the right proximal tibia was corrected by osteotomy in October of 1980. This osteotomy healed satisfactorily and the correction and position of his knee resulted in a secondary varus deformity of his right distal fibula. He was admitted for osteotomy of the right distal tibia to allow his foot to be placed plantigrade on the floor. His other problems are deformities of his femoral heads, dwarfing of his spine, lumbar and thoracolumbar scoliosis.


Physical examination:

On examination, he was a dwarfed boy with multiple deformities, very cheerful and intelligent. He had a short neck with a restricted range of motion in all planes.. The chest had an increased A.P. diameter. He had a left lumbosacral scoliosis and a right thoracic scoliosis with a thoracic rib hump. His spine was relatively shorter than his legs. Both elbows had crepitius and a 25 degree flexion deformity. The right hip and the left hip had a 15 and 25 degree flexion deformity respectively. However, the range of abduction and adduction and rotation of the hips was only reduced by a few degrees. The right knee had a five degree flexion deformity. There was a recent scar on the right proximal tibia. There was 20 degrees of residual valgus proximally in the right hip, however the distal right tibia had a 40 degree varus deformity and the foot was not able to be put plantigrade on the ground. Instead, he walked on the outside of his foot. The boy was still walking with a marked limp as he is in the rehabilitation stage following his proximal tibia osteotomy. The left proximal tibia was 15 degrees of valgus. Hands and feet were short and broad.

Course in hospital:

It was felt that this boy had spondyloepiphyseal dysplasia. On the 15th of January, he had a drill osteoclasis of the right tibia in the supram alleolart region. The bone was corrected manually and he was placed in a long leg plaster. He did well postoperatively and before long was ambulating with crutches.

194

He was discharged home to be followed in clinic in six weeks.

*Earl Bogosh, M.D.*

**Hospital for Sick Children**

**Surgical out-patient clinic**

**29 April 1981**

Shawn was reviewed clinically today and he looks pretty good. He still has a fair amount of valgus in his knee, but it is generally improved. His gait is improving, although he still limps minimally. He has good range of motion in his knee and his ankle.

He is to return to clinic in approximately nine months for clinical review at that time, he should have an orthoroentgenogram of his legs.

*E. Stanley, M.D.*

**Hospital for Sick Children**

**Surgical out-patient clinic**

**4 February 1982**

Shawn is now 11 years old with a diagnosis of spondyloepiphyseal dysplasia. He is 13 months status post proximal tibias osteogtomy for correction of valgus deformity of the knees followed by a distal tibial osteotomy to bring his foot plantigrade. He presents today with no specific complaints. He is participating in some school sports. He manages to walk the 300 yards from the bus stop to home without difficulty.

On physical examination, his gait indicates plantigrade right foot. However, there is marked valgus deformity of the right knee. His range of motion is good in both right knee and ankle.

His x-ray shows approximately 32 degrees of valgus of the right knee with good healing of the operative sites.

The patient was examined by Dr. Bobechko who felt that no further treatment is indicated at the present time. However, it is likely that he will need correction of deformities in the future. He was sent for photographs to be included in the chart. He will be seen back in clinic in one year's time.

*M. Heller, M.D.*

**Hospital for Sick Children**

**Discharge report**

**20 February 1983**

Final diagnosis – Spondyloepiphyseal dysplasia

Procedure – right proximal tibial osteotomy

This 13 year old boy with spondyloepiphyseal dysplasia presents with genu valgus. He has had previous osteotomies of the right tibia for valgus knee and varus ankle in 1980. He now has recurrence of this deformity. He says he gets occasional pain in the right ankle. He is able to walk several blocks with crutches.

Past medical history – also includes a fracture of his left femur. He has no allergies and is on no medications. He wears glasses.

Physical examination: He was a short obese 13 year old boy who was normocephalic. Head and neck was unremarkable. The chest was barrel-shaped but was clear with no crepitations or wheeze. There were normal heart sounds but no added sounds. The abdomen was obese but there was no organomegaly palpable. Examination of the arms revealed normal shoulders and the elbows had normal supination and pronation but a 20 degree fixed flexion deformity bilaterally. Hands and wrists appeared normal. Examination of the hips revealed a relatively normal range of motion. He had a 60 degree valgus deformity of his right knee with a 30 degree fixed flexion deformity. It was 135 degrees of total flexion. His left knee had 45 degrees of valgus again with a 30 degree fixed flexion deformity. Both feet were plantigrade.

He had 30 degrees of plantar flexion through the ankles and 30 degree was of dorsi flexion.

His post-operative course was uneventful, there were no problems with the cast. His leg remained intact neurovascularly. He complained of some pain at the osteotomy site. He was discharged home on 20 February 1983. No prescription was given. He will be re-admitted in six weeks for removal of his cast.

Future re-admission will have to be made for a distal tibial osteotomy to re-align the foot to put this plantigrade.

*J. Stewart, M.D.*

**Hospital for Sick Children**

**Discharge Report**

**13 May 1983**

Final diagnosis – Spondylo-epiphyseal dysplasia

Procedure: Right supra-malleolar tibial osteotomy performed on 9 May 1983

History of present illness: This 13 year-old male, who is known to have Morquio's disease, which was diagnosed when he was approximately two years old, has had no previous medical history.

Past surgical history includes a history of a fractured femur in September 1979. He has had a proximal osteotomy of the right tibia and fibula in October 1980 for a valgus knee. He has had a distal osteotomy of the right tibia in January 1981 for a varus tibia deformity. In February 1983 he had a closing medial wedge osteotomy of his proximal tibia for a valgus deformity of his knee and he is presently admitted to have a drill osteotomy of his distal tibia to correct the varus deformity of his ankle.

He was on no medication at the time of admission and had no known allergies. He lives at home with his parents. He is attending regular school.

Physical examination:

Head and neck revealed that he had a short neck with full range of motion. His chest was barrel shaped but otherwise clear to IPPA. CVS examinations revealed a pulse of 80 per minute which is regular and of normal volume. The heart sounds were normal, there were no added sounds and no murmurs.

Abdominal examination revealed that he was obese. The abdomen was soft and non tender, there was no organomegaly, no intraabdominal masses and the bowel sounds were normal.

Examination of the MSS revealed that he had a very short stature with short trunk and short limbs. He had a barrel chest, he had a thoracic kyphosis which was quite marked.

In terms of his hips, he had 135 degrees of flexion, 30 degrees of abduction, 20 degrees of adduction, 80 degrees of internal rotation, 45 degrees of external rotation and no fixed flexion contracture on the right side. He had essentially the same range on the left except that he had 60 degrees of external rotation instead of 45 degrees.

At the knees on the right, he had a 30 degree fixed flexion contracture on the left 10 degrees. The right knee had a range of motion from 30 degrees of fixed flexion to 160 degrees and on the left from 10 degrees to 160 degrees. He had 15 degrees of valgus deformity at his knees bilaterally.

He had a recurvatum and varus deformity of his distal right tibia. He had mild deformity of the distal left tibia. He stood with his right heel in marked varus and his left heel in moderate varus. Examination of the upper extremities revealed that he had quite short limbs. Examination of the shoulders, wrists and hands were normal. The elbows showed 20 degrees bilateral flexion contractures.

This child was taken to the operating room on 9 May 1982, where he underwent a drill osteotomy of the right distal tibia and fibula and the leg was positioned so as to bring the distal tibia out of varus. X-rays which were taken showed good position. He had a slight amount of recurvatum through the fracture site which was good because this tended to counteract the fixed flexion deformity of the knee which tended to have him walk with rather an equinous type of gait.

While he was here, his mother requested that he be seen by genetic service in terms of counselling for her and also for them to explain the disease process to the child as he was quite keen to learn about his disease.

He was seen by the genetic service who did rather extensive consultation and ordered a fairly extensive metabolic investigation.

A 24-hour urine study for keratosulphate was done. A cardiology consultation was also obtained and this showed no evidence of heart disease. Specifically, no evidence of aortic regurgitation was noted.

An ENT consult was asked for and he appeared to have normal hearing on clinical examination. However, audiometry was arranged. An ophthalmology consult was done and this showed that he had some evidence of corneal haze and no other obvious problems.

The child did quite well and when his urine collection was completed, he was discharged from  hospital.

The plan was to have him return to the orthopaedic clinic in six weeks time to have his cast off and x-rays taken. He was also to return to the metabolic clinic to see Dr. Lowden in four to six weeks at which time the results of his urine collection and so on will be back and the disease will be discussed with the family.

*T. Tanzer, M.D.*

**Hospital for Sick Children**

**Surgical out-patient clinic**

**24 June 1983**

This young man is six weeks since his supramalleolar osteotomy. He has just come out of his cast.  There is no area of localized tenderness. X-ray shows satisfactory healing is progressing. He will remain out of his cast and gradually mobilize and we will review him again in mid-August with x-ray of his right tibia on arrival.

*R. Wray, M.D.*

**Hospital for Sick Children**

**Surgical out-patient clinic**

**6 July 1983**

I saw Shawn in the clinic on Monday, July 4th. He had been referred after his last admission to the hospital for investigation of the nature of his spondyloepiphyseal dysplasia.

He is a thirteen-and-a-half-year-old boy, who had been followed at HSC since 1972. At age 2 he was noted to have a waddling gait and a lumbar lordosis. He was investigated extensively at that time and a radiologic diagnosis of spondyloepiphyseal dysplasia was made. In particular, it was noted that his urinary mucopolysaccharides were normal. It was also noted that bony disorder appeared to have some intermittent feature, that he had a strikingly abnormal pelvis and involvement of many growth plates and articular cartilage.

His intellect was normal and his development was normal.

Since that time he has been followed largely by your (Dr. Bobechko) service with many admissions to hospital in which he has been treated for a fractured femur, has had osteotomies, and most recently was discharged following supra-malleolar tibial osteotomy in May of this year.

During his admission he was seen by Rod McInnes in consultation, who suggested that a more intensive work-up of the nature of his inherited disease, was warranted.

On examination, he is a bright, pleasant young man. Only 120 cm in length, which places him at the 50$^{th}$ percentile for a 7 year old. His upper/lower ratio of 1.1 is abnormal, but not strikingly so. He has a short neck, barrel chest, mild scoliosis and a thoracic kyphosis. There is limitation of movement of several of his joints, particularly in his hips and knees, and he has a vargus deformity of his knees bilaterally. His fundi are normal. He has a slight hazyness of his cornea, but it is very mild for a child of his age. His ears are normal. His hearing appears normal. He has a faint systolic murmur maximal on the left sternal border. His blood pressure is 120/80. He has no organomegaly although his liver is palpable at the costal margin. His chest is somewhat scalloped and his liver does not appear large. He has no hernia. His hair is normal and his skin is slightly thickened but of normal texture.

Apart from the many abnormalities in his legs which you have been following, radiographs of his head and neck show marked displacement of C1 on C2 and a hypoplastic odontoid. His vertebrae are flattened in a typical manner for Morquio disease. Because of this I carefully examined his neurologic function, particularly in his upper limbs because children with Morquio disease are subject to gradual cord compression syndromes, which are often insidious in onset. He has normal power with slightly decreased tone in both upper and lower limbs. His tendon jerks are normal. His sensation is intact for pain, position sense and light touch. His fine motor movements are excellent.

In the laboratory we have measured his urinary mucopolysaccharides and find them in normal quantities as they had previously been demonstrated in 1972. More importantly, however, he does have keratan sulphate in his urine, which is distinctly abnormal and found only in children with Morquio disease. We have measured his leucocyte B—galactosidase which is normal and thus assume that he has a Morquio, Type A disease, although we have not yet measured his hexosamine sulfate sulfatase,

I spent considerable time talking to the family about the genetics of Morquio disease and the risks for other members of the family. I also talked to them about the prognosis for Shawn, and in particular, discussed the problems of cord compression syndromes. Because these are so common in teenage children with Morquio disease I think it is essential that he be followed on a regular basis and if at some point in the future he begins to develop soft neurological signs in his arms, that a stabilization procedure or laminectomy in the C1, C2, region be considered.

*J.A. Lowden, M.D., Ph.D*

The Research Institute

Hospital for Sick Children

**Hospital for Sick Children**

**Surgical out-patient clinic**

**29 October 1984**

This is a pleasant boy with spondyloepiphyseal dysokasia and extremely grotesque deformities of his lower extremities.

At present, when he walks he has a tremendous bilateral genu valgum. His hips are poor and his knees are poor and his ankles are poor and he is extremely short.

Radiographically, his growth is now complete.

I think this boy needs four separate distinct operative procedures.

The first would be to do a high right tibial osteotomy and swing his leg 45 degrees into varus.

This, of course, has the danger of peroneal nerve problems but there really is no alternative because he is going to drift into progressive valgus as time goes by. Approximately two months later, he could then have a supramalleolar osteotomy to swing his foot back into valgus to re-align his right leg.

Several months later a similar set of procedures will be done on his left leg.

Although this means four separate procedures, it means that he could be kept mobile on crutches whereas if the procedures were done bilaterally, such as a bilateral proximal tibial osteotomy, he would be stuck in a wheelchair for a 6 to 8 week period.

We have discussed all this with Shawn and his mother and his mother will be back in touch with us when they have made a decision as to whether they wish surgery and if so, when and if a decision is made to when, as to whether he wants it bilaterally or unilaterally as I would personally suggest.

*W.P. Bobechko, M.D. F.R.C.S.(C)*

**Hospital for Sick Children**

**Discharge Report**

**19 February 1985**

Admitting diagnosis:

Spondyloepiphyseal dysplasia

Shawn is a 15-year-old male, well known to Dr. Bobechko for previous osteotomies in his right lower limb. He is known to have Morquio's disease. He had deformities of his lower extremities mainly of the knees, genuvalgum and ankles. He has undergone right osteotomy times 2, but the right knee has progressively drifted in to valgus again.

He was admitted for bilateral osteotomy.

Past medical history:

Right osteotomy times 2. Right drill osteotomy times 2 as well.

On admission, he was not taking any medications. He was not allergic to any drugs. He did not smoke.

On physical examination, blood pressure was 128/90, pulse 103 per minute. Physical examination of the neck and head and ENT showed a short neck, otherwise normal.

Chest, barrel-shaped, increased AP diameter. Clear to auscultation. CVS was normal, Abdomen soft, non tender, no masses, no organomegally. Bowel sounds normal.

MSK – knees – bilateral genuvalgum, right 35 degrees, left 20 degrees. Range of motion – right 30-120, left 10-120. There was no effusion or tenderness. Ankles – both ankles were lax. We were able to manually subluxate both, more the right.

He was admitted and all preop tests were within normal limits. On February 14, 1985, he was taken to the o.r. for bilateral osteotomy. The postop course of this patient was unremarkable except for severe pain in the immediate postop period. The pain subsided in the following days and the neurovsculaar status was always normal.

This patient was discharged on February 19, 1985, to be seen in the Out-Patient Clinic in seven weeks time.

*L. Flores, M.D.*

**Hospital for Sick Children**

**Discharge report**

**12 May 1985**

Final diagnosis:

Epiphyseal dysplasia.

History:

15-year-old male with Morquio's. who was admitted for bilateral supra-malleolar, tibial osteotomies, due to varus deformation of both distal tibiae.

Past medical history was significant for bilateral proximal tibial osteotomies, varus, on February 14, 1985. On this occasion, it was the admission for second stage of the procedure, which was correction of the varus aspect of the distal tibia. The patient underwent bilateral drill osteotomies of the tibia and fibula with a correction of his varus deformity and application of long leg casts.

Post-operatively, his neurovascular status was stable and he was discharged in stable condition to be followed in clinic.

*M. Heller, M.D.*

# Shawn Brush

**Hospital for Sick Children**

**Surgical out-patient clinic**

**28 October 1985**


This 16-year-old boy with Morquio's syndrome has had proximal and tibial osteotomies bilaterally for his malalignments with multiple epiphyseal dysplasia. His only concerns now are from his shoe wear and right knee pain. The right knee gets stiff after he has been sitting for a long time and occasionally snaps when he pulls it out to a straight position.

On examination he walks with a significant abductor lurch bilaterally. He does have moderate knee flexion contractures bilaterally. He also has a residual genuvalgum with approximately 6 cms between his malleolae when his knees are touching. His spine is straight although he has an increased antral posterior diameter. He does have pain on patella femoral compression and his right patella is noted to subluxate as he extends it. Frank dislocation was not possible to demonstrate, and he does not recall this ever happened either.

X-rays today show that the alignment is much improved. We will see him back in one year and he should have clinical photographs done at that time. He should not need x-rays then.

In the meantime, we have also referred him for a teaching program through a physiotherapist for straight leg arising.


*A. Smith, M.D.*


**Hospital for Sick Children**

**Surgical out-patient clinic**

**12 November 1986**


This 17-year-old male has Morquio's syndrome which was disagnosed after many years of investigations. He has had proximal and distal tibial osteotomies and varus deformity of both ankles and valgus deformities of both knees.

His gait has improved and he thinks that there is no instability of his knees and the right knee tends to become stiffer than the left.

He was also wondering about his neck as he had read that Morquios often have neck instability.

On examination he has a good range of motion of his neck with forward flexion limited by his barrel chest. There is no pain and he is neurologically intact which would not suggest that he has significant subluxation of C1 and C2.

His right knee has a 30 degree flexion contracture but is stable and extends to neutral. There is valgus instability but he has some anterior laxity bilaterally. The overall alignment, when he walks, is adequate.

X-rays reveal that he does have significant C1 and C2 subluxation and this is due to a hypoplastic odontoid. He has been warned not to participate in heavy activity that might cause a sudden flexion injury to his neck. The x-rays of his leg show good overall alignment of his hip dysplasia which has not been treated.

We will see him again in one year's time.


*C. Young, M.D.*


**Hospital for Sick Children**

**Surgical out-patient clinic**

**11 January 1988**


This 18-year-old male with Morquio's syndrome was seen today for his annual visit. He has no major complaints and does not desire any further orthopaedic intervention at the present time.

We have some discussion with his mother concerning his feet and they mentioning that they had thought about having custom shoes made. In addition, there is a leg length discrepancy and these are approximately 1 ½ cm short on the right side.

We discussed using a felt insert to see if this young man would benefit from an orthosis or an augmentation of the sole of the shoe.

The patient seemed to be happy to proceed along this course before trying any custom shoes or orthoses.

As this patient is from, Burlington, they felt that it would be better for them to have their Family Practitioner coordinate further orthopedic consultation.


*P.C. Missiuna, M.D.*

## 25

# Quotes that inspire Shawn

"Fate shuffles the cards and we play."

*Arthur Schopenhauer (1788-1860); German Philosopher.*

"A person often meets his destiny on the road he took to avoid it."

*Jean de La Fontaine (1621-1695); French poet.*

"We are not permitted to choose the frame of our destiny. But what we put into it is ours."

*Dag Hammarskjöld (1905-1961); Swedish statesman*

"The reward of a thing well done is to have done it."

*Ralph Waldo Emerson (1803-1882); U.S. philosopher, poet.*

"If at first you don't succeed, try, try again."

*Robert Bruce(1274-1329); King of Scotland.*

*( The name "Brush" comes from the Bruce)*

"Great souls have wills; feeble ones have only wishes."

*Chinese proverb.*

.

"The art of winning is learned in defeat."

*Simon Bolivar (1783-1830); Venezuelan soldier, politician and writer.*

"The time for action is now. It's never too late to do something."

*Antoine de Saint-Exupery (1900-1944); French aviator and writer.*

"I prefer the folly of enthusiasm to the indifference of wisdom."

*Anatole France (1844-1924); French author.*

Everyone has talent. What is rare is the courage to follow the talent to the dark place where it leads.

*Erica Jong.*

"...what the thinker thinks the prover will prove"

*- Prometheus Rising; R A Wilson.*

"It does not matter how slowly you go, so long as you do not stop."

*Confucius (551-479 BC); Chinese philosopher.*

"Mistrust first impulses; they are nearly always good."

*Charles-Maurice de Talleyrand (1754-1838); French statesman.*

"The beginning is the most important part of the work."

*Plato (428-347 BC); Greek philosopher.*

"Next to knowing when to seize an opportunity, the most important thing in life is to know when to forego an advantage."

*Benjamin Disraeli (1804-1881); English politician, novelist.*

"Avoid delays: procrastination always does harm."

*Marcus Annaeus Lucanus (39-65 AD); Roman poet.*

"It's not what you look at that matters, it's what you see."

*Henry David Thoreau (1817 - 1862); U.S. essayist, poet.*

"The beginning and the end are shared in the circumference of the circle."

*Heraclitus (544-480 BC); Greek philosopher.*

"To improve is to change; to be perfect is to change often."

*Sir Winston Churchill (1874-1965); English statesman.*

"The palest of ink is better than the best memory."

*Chinese proverb.*

"In order to succeed, we must first believe that we can."

*Nikos Kazantzakis (1855-1957); Greek writer.*

"Simplicity is nature's first step, and the last of art."

*Philip James Bailey (1816 - 1902); English poet.*

"Bad art is a great deal worse than no art at all."

*Oscar Wilde (1854-1900); Anglo-Irish playwright, author.*

"There must be something strangely sacred in salt: it is found in our tears and in the sea."

*Gibran, Khalil (1883-1931); Lebanese essayist, novelist and poet.*

.

"If the wind will not serve, take to the oars."

*Latin proverb.*

"We cannot cross the sea merely by staring at the water."

*Rabindranath Tagore (1861-1941); Indian poet, writer, philosopher.*

"Confidence is that feeling by which the mind embarks in great and honorable courses with a sure hope and trust in itself."

*Marcus Tullius Cicero (106 - 3 BC); Roman statesman, scholar, orator.*

"The pessimist sees difficulty in every opportunity. The optimist sees the opportunity in every difficulty."

*Winston Churchill (1874 - 1965); English statesman, author.*

"Nothing in the world is more dangerous than sincere ignorance and conscientious stupidity."

*Martin Luther King, Jr. (1929 - 1968); U.S. civil rights leader.*

"Doubt is not a pleasant condition, but certainty is an absurd one."

*Voltaire - born Francois-Marie Arouet (1694-1778); French writer.*

"An experience is never a failure because it always serves to show something."

*Thomas Alva Edison (1847-1931); U.S. physicist and inventor.*

"Fire tries gold, misery tries brave men."

*Lucius Annaeus Seneca (2 BC - 65 AD); Roman philosopher.*

"Experience is not what happens to a man; it is what a man does with what happens to him."

*Aldous Huxley (1894-1963); English critic, novelist.*

"Happiness depends upon ourselves."

*Aristotle (384 - 322 BC); Greek writer, philosopher.*

"Everything can be bought in society, except character."

*Marie Henri Beyle Stendhal (1783-1842); French novelist.*

"Little things console us because little things afflict us."

*Blaise Pascal (1623-1662); French mathematician.*

"There is no road or ready way to virtue."

*Thomas Browne (1605-1682); English physician, writer.*

"Vitality shows in not only the ability to persist  but the ability to start over."

*F. Scott Fitzgerald (1896-1940); U.S. author.*

"We are all in the gutter, but some of us are looking at the stars."

*Oscar Wilde.*

"We make the path by walking."

*Antonio Machado (1875-1939); Spanish poet.*

"For the things we have to learn before we can do them, we learn by doing them."

*Aristotle (384-322 BC); Greek philosopher.*

"Do not say a little in many words, but a great deal in a few."

*Pythagoras (570-500 BC); Greek philosopher.*

"From a certain point onward there is no longer any turning back. That is the point that must be reached."
*Franz Kafka (1883-1924); Czech writer.*

"Fortunately, somewhere between chance and mystery lies imagination."

*Luis Buñuel (1900-1983); Spanish filmmaker.*

"When one paints an ideal, one does not need to limit one's imagination."

*Ellen Key (1849-1926); Swedish author.*

"No one ever approaches perfection except by stealth, and unknown to themselves."

*William Hazlitt (1778-1830); English essayist.*

"Obscurity and competence: That is the life that is worth living."

*Mark Twain (1835-1910); U.S. author.*

"One's past is what one is. It is the only way by which people should be judged."

*Oscar Wilde (1854-1900); Anglo-Irish playwright.*

"Posterity weaves no garlands for imitators."

*Friedrich Von Schiller (1759-1805); German dramatist.*

"The fall of dropping water wears away the stone."

*Lucretius (99-55 BC); Roman poet, philosopher.*

"Results are what you expect, and consequences are what you get."

*Origin unknown.*

"Good lies need a leavening of truth to make them palatable."

*William Mcilvanney (b. 1936); British novelist.*

"The reasonable man adapts himself to the world; the unreasonable one persists in trying to adapt the world to himself."

*George Bernard Shaw (1856-1950)Anglo-Irish playwright, critic.*

"I can believe the impossible, but not the improbable."

*Gilbert Keith Chesterton (1874-1936); English writer.*

"The best fire does not flare up the soonest."

*George Eliot (1819-1880); Englist novelist.*

"You are sure to get anywhere, if you only walk long enough."

*Lewis Carrol (1832-1898); English author.*

"A man travels the world over in search of what he needs, and returns home to find it."

*George Moore (1852-1933); Irish author, poet, dramatist.*

"Words are wise men's counters, they do but reckon by them: but they are the money of fools."

*Thomas Hobb (1588-1679); English philosopher.*

"In the process of writing, memory and imagination are confused."

*Adelaida García Morales (1945); Spanish writer*

.

"I haven't understood a bar of music in my life, but I've felt it."

*Igor Feodorovich Stravinsky (1882-1971); Russian composer.*

"Johnny Cash, Bill Monroe, Tammy Wynette and Waylon Jennings all told me that it's not cool to name drop!!"

*Shawn Brush (1969- ) Canadian songwriter.*

# 26

# DISCOGRAPHY

To find out more about Shawn Brush visit his website for the most up-to-date information including news, photos, touring dates and merchandise,

# www.shawnbrush.com.

# 1995

*In The Land of Giants*

# 1998

*The Adrian Gail*

# 1999

*Plus Handling and Shipping*

# 2000

*Steal Town*

# 2001

*Kutz*

# 2002

*MIA*

# Shawn Brush

# 2003

*Youaskedforit*

# 2003

## *Shawn Brush and Friends*

# 2005

## *Bootlegs*

# 2006
## (Re-released as a CD)

*The Wooden Hill*

# 2007

*The Krooked Cowboy*
*Rides Again*

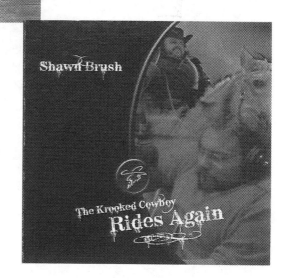

# Early cassettes from Shawn 1993-96

1994 . . . 1,000 cassettes made

1993 . . . 100 cassettes made

shawn brush
the crooked cowboy
LIVE at the
STAIRCASE THEATRE
Saturday October 25, 2003
27 Dundurn Street North
Hamilton, Ontario
905.529.3000
info@staircase.org
www.shawnbrush.com

shawn brush
LIVE at the
STAIRCASE THEATRE
$17.50 Canadian

John Farrington photo

*If you made it this far, congratulations.*

*The book has been a great experience for me.*

*I learned a lot about myself in the process.*

*If you have any questions or concerns please feel free to contact me.*

**www.shawnbrush.com**

## THE KROOKED COWBOY

April 2009